Cover Art Courtesy of Mary Longman

Before and After, 1991

Gatherings VI

"Metamorphosis"

Manifesting and Respecting
Diversity In Our Transformation

Theytus Books Ltd.
Penticton, BC

GATHERINGS:
The En'owkin Journal of First North American Peoples
Volume VI - 1995

Published annually by the Theytus Books Ltd. and the En'owkin
Centre for the En'owkin International School of Writing
Canadian Cataloguing in Publication Data
Gatherings
Annual
ISSN   1180-0666   ISBN 0-919441-80-7

1. Canadian literature (English)--Indian authors--Periodcals.
2. Canadian literature (English)--20th century--Periodicals.
3. American literature--Indian authors--Periodicals.
4. American literature--20th century--Periodicals.
I. En'owkin International School of Writing.
II. En'owkin Centre.
PS8235   C810.8'0897   CS90-31483-7

Managing Editors:	Don Fiddler and Linda Jaine
Associate Editors:	Gerry William, Greg Young-Ing
	Jeannette Armstrong
Page Composition:	Marlena Dolan, Regina Gabriel
Proofreading:	Regina Gabriel, Nancy Bomberry
	Armand Garnet Ruffo
Cover Design:	Marlena Dolan
Cover Art:	Mary Longman

Please send submissions and letters to 'Gatherings', c/o En'owkin Centre,
257 Brunswick Street, Penticton, B.C. V2A 5P9 Canada. All submissions
must be accompanied by self-addressed stamped envelope (SASE). Manuscripts without SASEs may not be returned. We will not consider previously
published manuscripts or visual art.

Typeset by Theytus Books Ltd. Printed and bound in Canada

*The publisher acknowledges the support of the Canada Council, Department
of Communications and the Cultural Services Branch of the Province of
British Columbia in the publication of this book.*

Table of Contents

Transition

Alteration

Conversion

Children

Introduction

At first impression he seemed forlorn. Standing awkwardly, dressed in faded blue jeans and a tattered old shirt that once might have been plaid, he looked out of place in comparison to the gleam of the office furniture. It would have been easy to dismiss him, as he hesitantly asked for help in a low toned broken English, head bowed and submissive. Another vagrant? There were many others seemingly like him, shadowing in the hidden corners of cites everywhere, men who seemed to have let life overwhelm them; who found solace, comfort and forgetfulness in whatever drugs of choice were available at the moment.

An elderly woman approached and spoke gently to him in the soft tones of the Okanagan language. Instantly there was a transformation! His glance moved upwards, his voice became stronger and clearer, and he seemed to grow taller as his tongue twisted around the familiar sounds of his youth. No longer was he an unwilling observer at the fringes of an imposed culture. Through the intertwined sounds of a seldom used language, he was reuniting once again to his grandfather, and his grandfather before him.

In similar ways, using a new language, contemporary Aboriginal writers experience the transformational power of story. Through the act of writing our culture is recreated,, strengthened, regenerated and eventually transmitted. Languages link people to the past, to the roots of their being, and build bridges from the depths of their ancestry to the present. Language is inexorably linked to culture, which is linked to self respect, which is linked to empowerment. And so the circle goes.

Knowledge and understanding are powerful tools of humankind and only through clear and accurate communication, the survival tools of culture, can First Nations people be empowered. Even as you read this, our writers are exploring new ways, articulating new ideas, creating contemporary culture. The stories within this volume of Gatherings speak to transformation, to empowerment, and to new beginnings.

Don Fiddler and Linda Jaine

Transition

Lonely
Metaphors
Are Story-less Figures

What's it worth
to play charades
and look for
the wishing
rock?
At an Indian assembly,
a relative is talkin' Indian,
and feelin' good about bein' mad,
mad at those who don't understand.
He did have to shift
so all would know and
remember how babies talk.

mat swit i xn numt
Do you know what
I am saying?

Wanna hear about mountains?
"Noble-majestic-great-epic."
Beautiful words? original? mine?
You see, I learned 'em from books.
We've so many people with wonder
in their voices--and yet

there are so few
gifted translators.

and that's why I look
for the wishing rock
and play charades.

How'll You Understand

I am here realizing art never before seen using paint wiped from
  faces of Hollywood actors, and
I am here dancing in gymnasiums wearing orange and pink store-
  bought feathers, and
I am here listening to missionaries in 1652 and on the corner of
  5th Street and 3rd Avenue, and
I am here drinking cherry wine or after-shave lotion I pocketed
  from London Drugs, and
I am here objecting to classification systems which logically
  presume objects can't argue, and
I am here visiting my kids after finding I can fuck better than
I can be domestic, and
I am here sharing stories my grandmother told while making me
  rag doll toys, and
I am here watching videos of made-up Indians getting cut down by
  made-up heroes, and
I am here bumming loonies so I can sleep peacefully in the drunk
  tank, and
I am here dying of TB, AIDS, VD, OD and paying for it with BC,
  PEI, AB, NWT, and
I am here being molested by a priest who prays for my temporal
  deliverance, and
I am here forming poems in air and on paper with others denied
  entrance to the UN, and
I am here watching you follow me suspiciously when I shop for
  advertised specials, and
I am here walking barefoot in the first snow and smiling at my
  power, and
I am here mourning because my neighbour shot himself with the gun
I sometimes borrow, and
I am here learning to modern-dance with people from Berlin,
  Nairobi, and Peking, and
I am here studying theories of academics about why their people
  hate me, and
I am here bantering with the red-headed woman who says we stole
  bannock from Scotland, and
I am here singing honour songs at pow-wows and reading karaoke
  half pissed, and

I am here hitch-hiking to town on a Friday night to either get
   fucked or get in a fight, and
I am here wondering if I should feel anger instead of confusion
   when I experience racism, and
I am here sweating and springing into the lake through a hole I
   chopped in the ice, and
I am here laughing at ethnic jokes told by a Black comedian in a
   red leather suit, and
I am here reading hate-literature you wrote about me even though
I thought I wasn't noticed, and
I am here respecting your beauty and believing you will learn
   to appreciate mine, and
I am here ingesting your insults and I'm grateful that my colon
   functions properly, and
I am here fishing salmon in 1849 and taking one from the freezer
   to thaw for tomorrow, and
I am here remembering everything and everyone that happened and
   re-creating myself continuously

Joshua and the Troop Leader

One

Eric saw that the hood of the van was open in Stanley's driveway. Stanley was bent over the engine, struggling to get closer to the motor than his great belly would allow him. Eric called out, "Hey Stan, get that carburetter fixed yet?"

Stanley shot an irritable look at Eric and wiped his hands on an oily rag. "Not yet. Damn thing keeps stalling out when I hit thirty."

"Why don't you just take it to a mechanic?"

"You crazy? I'd rather take a hundred dollar bill and set it on fire right here," Stanley retorted. "I'll get it yet. Probably just the choke valve or something."

"Well, good luck anyway, Stan. You using this van to take the boy scouts out this weekend?"

"Only if you'll let me get back to work."

"Should I get my boy ready then?"

"Yeah, yeah," Stanley grumbled.

"O.K., we'll be at home then." Eric continued on to his house. His son, Joshua, in a crisp, clean boy scout uniform, was sitting on the porch, sharpening his new hatchet. It came with a carrying case that attached to a belt, and it had two pockets on it-one for a sharpening stone and the other Joshua used to hold some rabbit snares.

"Got your gear ready, son? I saw Stan up at his place getting the van ready." Eric paused for a second, "But he might not get it going. But get ready anyway."

"Alright Dad," replied Joshua. He slid the hatchet in the case attached to his waist and ran inside the house.

Eric smiled as he watched his son disappear through the screen door. He didn't have to worry about Josh, not since Josh started hanging out with his grandfather. You couldn't keep Josh out of the woods now. Eric's dad always brought Josh with him when he went out spearing eels or checking the trapline. Eric noticed how much happier both Dad and Josh seemed to be since Dad retired and took up the life of a woodsman once again.

Eric was brought out of his thoughts by the familiar rumble of Stanley's van as it came down the road. There were six other boys in the van, all dressed up in boy scout uniforms.

Two

"Hey Josh," Eric yelled as he went into the house to help Joshua with his gear, "the van's here." Eric grabbed a knapsack and brought it out to the van. He looked at Stanley, "Got the carburetter fixed, huh?"

"Nah, but I'll be O.K. as long as I don't go over thirty."

Joshua came out the door with is pup-tent and grub. He sprang into the van with his other friends. Meanwhile, Stanley got out, walked around to the front of the van and popped the hood. He had a big wrench in one hand and he began to beat on the carburetter. "Sticky choke valve. Maybe that will loosen it up some," he said.

'Where you taking them, Stan?" Eric asked.

"You know that old logging road that goes up to the ridge..."

"Yeah, but that's pretty swampy ground-especially this time of year."

Stanley shot a condescending look at Eric, "Not when you get up to the ridge. I hunt there every year."

Stanley was the administrative manager for the tribal council, so he didn't get to go outdoors much. But he always looked forward to the hunting season each fall, even though he definitely was not an outdoorsman. Stanley always made sure that he brought a skilled hunter with him, so he would stand a better chance of bringing home a prized trophy. This stint as a boy scout leader was only to boost his public image as a man of the woods.

"I might be out that way tomorrow," Eric added.

"Don't worry Eric. I'll take good care of your boy."

"Gotta pick up some ash for axe handles," Eric reassured Stanley.

"I'll probably see you up there then. And don't worry about Joshua. I know that ridge like the back of my hand."

Eric cautioned, "Well, take it easy. That ridge is forty miles out that road and if anything should happen..."

"Hey, we have to get going if we're going to get there by dark," Stanley interrupted as he turned to get in the van.

Three

The road up to the ridge was pretty sloppy. The spring rains were relentless and the deep ruts were filled with muddy water. The weatherman had said that the weekend would be clear and sunny, which was why Stanley had chosen this weekend for the camp-out, but the weatherman is right only half the time, and he sure wasn't right about his forecast this time.

The swamp which bordered the old logging road was flooded and it came only inches from covering the road itself. The rain began to fall heavily as they turned onto the logging road.

Inside the van, the heater was turned on full, driving away the damp chill of the spring air. The boys were oblivious to the dreary conditions outside. Joshua was glad his cousins were there—Lloyd and Carl. Then there was Kevin and Russell—two boys Joshua knew from school and played with at times. Of course there was Kenny, Stanley's boy, and the chief's son, Marlow. They were all looking forward to the camping trip and they chattered excitedly.

The entourage was about twenty-five miles out when the van skidded off the logging road, into a water-filled ditch. The van became hopelessly mired within seconds. Stanley let out a long tirade of obscenities as he shifted the gears from forward to reverse and back again in an effort to rock the van free, but it was obviously futile. The van was stuck.

"Alright boys, get out there and see if you can push me out," Stanley ordered.

"But the ditch is full of water," complained Marlow.

"Well, do you want to be stuck out here all night long?" Stanley snapped.

"Jeepers creepers! I'd better get my good deed badge for this!"

The boys crawled out of the van into knee-deep water. They stood there in the pouring rain, grimacing visibly. Inside the van, the temperature light on the dash lit up, indicating that the engine was beginning to overheat, due to the constant revving of the engine; but Stanley ignored it. Had he known that he damaged the carburetter when he hammered it with the wrench, and that gasoline was now spewing over the hot engine, he would have shut the engine down immediately. But he was just as frustrated as the boys and he continued to gun the engine. Smoke began to pour out from under the hood, and seconds later flames leapt out from the grill.

"Fire!" Stanley yelled as he dashed from the van, tripped and landed face-down in the ditch. He barely had time to get wet when he sprang up and scrambled away to safety. "Get away from the van," he shrieked. "Hurry!"

The boys just stood there, dumbstruck, as they gaped at the flames shooting from the engine.

"Goddammit!" Stanley screamed from the distance, "I said get away!"

Snapped out of their trance, the boys scurried away from the van. There was nothing they could do but stand there at a distance and helplessly watch the van burn. Within half-an-hour, the van was completely gutted, along with all of their gear.

"What are we going to do now?" Kenny asked in a shaky voice.

"We'll have to walk back," was the only thing Stanley could think of.

"But its getting dark and I'm cold," whined Marlow.

Stanley didn't know what to do. He was beginning to wish that he had stayed at home and watched the hockey finals on T.V., with an ice-cold beer in his hand. Standing in the pouring rain, twenty-five miles from nowhere, somehow made the whole idea of being back in the comfort of his own home seem so remote and unreal. They didn't have transportation, shelter, food...not even an axe. Like the rest of the boys, Stanley was cold and wet; and he didn't feel like walking the whole night in the rain. What they needed right away was a fire.

Deciding to make a fire, Stanley began to collect the sticks which were lying on the ground. The wood was saturated and despite Stanley's efforts to light them up, they simply would not catch on fire. He cursed at the top of his lungs and kicked the pile of sticks away.

"I know how to start a fire."

Four

Joshua immediately became self-conscious as everybody turned around to see that it was he who had spoken. Flustered as he was, Joshua could only comment on the most obvious, "We need dry wood."

Joshua knew that because of the wet spring, all of the wood lying on the ground would be as wet as a sponge. His grandfather had shown him how to find dry wood in a situation like this.

Joshua quickly scanned his surroundings until he spotted what he was looking for. He pointed to a thicket of young maple trees. They were about four inches in diameter. Three of the young trees in the cluster did not have any buds on them and their bark was hanging in shreds. Joshua knew that these trees were dead and would be dry on the insides. "There's some dry wood."

Joshua still had his hatchet with him and he began to chop the dead maples down. He then cut them up into firewood lengths and split them.

Kevin picked one of the split pieces and examined it. "Hey, this wood's dry!" he announced.

Joshua continued to split some of his wood until they were about the thickness of a pencil. The rest he left as halves and quarters. He then peeled some birchbark from a nearby tree and stacked the pencil-sized pieces of wood on top of it. The fire caught immediately when a match was put to it. Joshua waited until the fire was well established before he put the larger pieces of wood on it.

Feeling more confident in himself, Joshua announced, "We'll need some shelter from the rain. We need some lean-to's."

Joshua cut some spruce saplings and arranged them into a ramp-like framework. On the ramp of the frame, he placed more saplings horizontally and parallel to each other, spacing them about two feet apart. He fastened these saplings with everybody's donated shoelaces.

Joshua explained as he was tying the saplings, "Usually you'd use spruce roots, but modern stuff has its uses-saves time, too."

Next, Joshua went to a nearby stand of fir trees and began to break off boughs about three feet long. The other boys, sensing that Joshua had some kind of purpose for these boughs, began to do likewise.

Joshua noticed that the boys were breaking the boughs off indiscriminately, in lengths varying from six inches to two feet. "No. We need them this long," Joshua corrected the boys, showing them a bough from his bundle.

As the scout troop was busily collecting fir boughs, Joshua began to thatch the roof of the lean-to he had made. He snapped off a sprig at the thick end of the fir boughs, leaving a hooklike feature. Joshua hung these boughs by their hooks across the lowest sapling, lashed horizontally across the back of the lean-to.

The boy scouts returned with a great supply of fir boughs, just as Joshua was beginning the row directly about the first row. The second row overlapped the first row by a foot. The third row likewise overlapped the second row, and so on, until Joshua had reached the top.

"See how the rain runs down the upper row of boughs," Joshua demonstrated. "When it gets to the next row it keeps running down, to the next rows until it runs off onto the ground at the back. Neat, huh? You guys want to try one. We might need two lean-to's."

Joshua supervised the boys' progress as they avidly worked on the second lean-to. The work was finished and Joshua seemed satisfied with the craftsmanship.

"My grandfather uses cedar boughs for the floor," Joshua commented and he began to gather some. "We're going to need more firewood, too, for the whole night."

Within minutes, the boy scouts demonstrated how well they had learned their lessons, when they brought back armloads of dry, seasoned hardwood. The boys were laughing and beginning to look like they were enjoying themselves.

Stanley, who had been sullen throughout the entire situation and who had done nothing but squat by the fire, warming his hands, abruptly rose to his feet and declared, "We're still twenty-five miles from nowhere. What are we going to eat, how are we going to get back?"

Instinctively, the boys turned to Joshua. Joshua smiled and said, "My Dad's coming by tomorrow, but if you guys want some rabbits for breakfast, I'll set up a few snares right now. I saw a few nice rabbit trails back there. I'll guarantee at least two by morning."

"Yeah!" the boys declared unanimously, gathering around Joshua, eager to learn the next lesson in wood lore.

The Rhythm of Letting Go

From the river bank
we watch the salmon struggle.
So many eyes trained on the flash,
the surge of silver and fin.
They turn upstream
torn and ragged,
hollow-eyed and yellow
in the cold November sun.
On the river's edge,
I kiss you one last time.
We have come back to knowing
we can't hold each other any more.

Small Stories Of Mixed Blood

"Marry a white man and you'll have everything."

My mother learned to listen too well
to Sister Dodo's* teachings
at St. Mary's Residential School.
Mom's status stripped at her first wedding,
she became a Finnish Subject
without ever knowing.
My father was her second husband
from across the cold ocean.

My grandfather danced down Main street,
red and yellow feathers
bright against his brown skin,
his mocassined feet stepping
lightly on the hot summer pavement,
my small feet, already trained
in the five positions of ballet
tapping each drum beat,
the rhythm reaching into my stomach
pulling me from the sidewalk.
My father's pale hand held me back.

Daddy told his friends
Mom had blue blood,
him being Aryan and all,
they accepted his excuse,
said she was too pretty
to be any old squaw.
He cut the plug from the t.v.
when Barbara Streisand sang,
put it back with black tape
for CBC specials on W.W. II,
he'd bark at us in German,
tell us how it really was.

Mom grew paler over the years,
an unseen leech bleeding colour
from her cheeks each Saturday night
when Daddy drove us downtown,
pointed at the drunks waddling
from bar to bar; at the kid waiting on the curb
with a bag of chips, a bottle of orange crush.
He told her she wasn't like them,
shook his finger and told me how lucky I was.
Daddy bought her booze to drink at home,
stashed his under the porch stairs.
He'd be sober when she woke up;
Mama still craved the sweet wine.

At school I heard talk of Indians
in from a good week's fishing,
they'd fight for their weekend catch,
someone swinging a 2x4 like a war club,
both men and women scrapping
on the street called Apache Pass.*
My wide-eyed white friends
said I wasn't like them.
I hid Mom's bottles, kept her inside
so they wouldn't see her staggering.

The white boys whispered
about hot-blooded, half-breed girls.
Teddy B. figured he'd try taking me
behind the bushes at the park.
He told his friends how I opened my legs,
offering myself against the tree,
how I was dark all over and oh, so easy,
the white girls sneered,
how could I at thirteen?
I lowered my eyes and bit my lips,
let them spread their stories.

I went searching for myself,
the pack heavy on my back.

My cousins called me apple,
said my green eyes were like go lights
flashing at the good looking drummers.
They told me mooniaquay were loose.
Indian women are modest,
so I lowered my eyes and spent
the next ten years wandering,
wishing for shiny black braids.

I came home and found my mother
praying to Jesus in Ojibway,
lying in the dingy bedroom
the chemo's venom in her veins,
the light strained through the drapes
giving her face a pale green tinge.
I knew the cancer leech
was bloated with Mama's red blood.
Daddy started burning her things
before she was dead; the fire was small.

At thirty, I sat on the shoulders
of Bear Butte watching the storm
roll closer across the open plains.
With every lightning strike
I cried for my grandfather,
offering tobacco as each foot
touched down beside me,
the drum in my chest beating.
In this black light I knew
the colour of my skin.

*Sister Dodo=Mom always talked about Sister Dondot..I thought it was
"Dodo". As well as being an extinct bird species, dodo also means "teat"
in Ojibway.
*Apache Pass=Famous section of lower third avenue in Prince Rupert.
*Mooniaquay=White woman.
*Bear Butte=Ceremonial fasting grounds, S. Dakota.

Aloha Ojibwa

August, it was, and Sunday, the Kaministikwia River drifting wide and gentle past the front gate of Ontario's Old Fort William. Inside the palisades, on a dampish patch of lawn, fifteen men and women sat crosslegged on a circle of Hudson's Bay blankets. They had just begun the Ojibwa purification ceremony at Keeshigun, the annual Ojibwa weekend celebration at the living history fur-trade era fort.

I had come the day before, a writer on vacation, peeking 200 years into the past. I live in Oregon, far from Ontario, equally far from my ancestors' Pacific homeland, where I was born. Today my travelling companion opted for church, and I returned to Old Fort William alone, thinking to catch the demonstration of canoe-building, to converse with voyageurs and clarks.

The dance ground of the day before, where I had seen a regal man in purple and a younger Ojibwa in striking black and white, lay quiet in the early morning. On the nearby lawn, slightly inside the blanket circle, a small woman intoned something too softly for me to hear. I stepped closer. A man beckoned me to one remaining seat on the grass.

I sat, removed my sandals. What to do now? I had meant to be an observer. To my left sits the purple warrior from the dance, now wearing jeans and a crumpled white cotton shirt. Before him on the ground, grasses smoulder in an abalone shell. He whooshes the smoke over his head, around his body. Then he leans, whispers to me: "Remove your jewellery to smudge."

My insides churn like the volcanic middle earth, reminding me how I hate well meaning but ignorant strangers appropriating my people's ceremonies, how I despise arrogant tourists denigrating our ancient gods. What to do? Clearly the warrior expects me to "smudge."

My rings stick. I lick my finger, force the first ring over my knuckle. The bowl of smoke passes around the entire circle clockwise, back to me. I don't know what to do. I look to my new friend. He just nods. I lean over, inhaling cautiously. To my surprise, the smoke is calming. I turn my hands over it, as if drying them. I waft the smoke toward my face and hand the bowl to my friend. It feels like a chalice.

The bowl passes back to the elder leading the group. She smudges last, "as a sign that no one is better than any other." Those who are Christian, she says, may recite the Lord's prayer in Ojibwa. A few people do. She opens the circle to other prayers, exhorts us to include all people in our supplications, tells us that's why Indians refer to four colours, for all the people of the earth. She says it is up to us to set things right.

In the silence, an axe splitting firewood rings out from across the fort's main square. To my right, a white man prays for the black birch dying from acid rain. A woman across the circle confesses how embarrassed she is to be white, how she carries the sins of the fathers. My friend on my left prays: "I thank the Great Spirit for the gift of sight to see the beauty of the Earth, for the gift of smell...the gift of hearing...I thank the Great Spirit for the privilege of having a family to care for."

To me his English words from his Ojibwa heart are like new fire under a full kettle. I think of how I renounced Christianity long ago, of meeting an old Mohawk chief some years later. He looked at me carefully and said, "What are you? I see in your eyes you must go back to your people." Now, at words from another Indian, the reservoir that is my heart bursts. My eyes fill with tears. My nose begins to drip, but I dare not wipe it. And then, almost choking, I do something I have not done since I was a Sunday School child: I pray by myself out loud. "I pray for my people," I begin. "Who are Hawaiian. I pray for my people, the people of all the Earth. I pray that we let the Earth heal us, that we in turn might heal the Earth." I have finished. I try not to sniffle.

The elder looks up. "Thank you," she says. "Thank you." She and two young Indian men flanking her take up rattles, and sing in Ojibwa. The ceremony is over.

My new friend, the purple warrior, speaks. Vernon Kimball, a name as Indian as mine is Hawaiian, a name because our grandmothers or our grandmothers' grandmothers married white men who came to their lands. Vernon wants to know about Hawaiians. I tell him how I go home twice a year to learn, to write about my people. He asks if I would speak a few words at the dance in the afternoon. I am a writer, not a speaker. I sweat fear thinking about how large the crowd was yesterday. Hundreds, maybe a thousand.

Once, years ago, I spoke to a group of 50, rattled for days before and after. I swallow hard, and I think "no." And then I hear myself say, "Of course."

Vernon says, "I have to go now. I'll find you later. Let you know." He disappears across the lawn. No time, no place, I'm off the hook, I think. Good. I spoke my piece in the prayer.

In the afternoon the sun beats down and the drums begin. Six singers wail in a center shade pavilion. Dancers of America's First Nations wind around the circle in waving ranks, moccasined toes keeping the rhythm, point-step,point-step. I am squeezed among the spectators. Around the curve comes the young man I'd seen yesterday in the dance with Vernon. Three-fourths of his face is painted white. His long black hair flows over his white bone breastplate. Eagle feathers on his head and back fan with power, black leggings are striped in white.

Vernon steps out of the dance, leans toward me and says "Come." I follow. He introduces me to the announcer, who says "in five minutes, at the end of this song."

Vernon takes my hand and lays it open. "I have the traditional gift for you." He lays a pinch of tobacco in my palm, and slides back into the dance. The tobacco is a light rusty brown, fine in texture. I close my hand over it and with my fist I press a little tablet against my leg. With my other hand I write some notes. My pen struggles. What will I say? My handwriting careens nervously over the small page. I hear my name on the speakers. My heart thumps like the drums, my perspiring hand clutches the tobacco.

"Aloha. I am native Hawaiian." My voice comes from the speakers clearly, slowly. I feel like I have unwrapped in front of what seems the whole world a secret I should never have kept. People listen. "I bring greetings to all of you and especially the Ojibwa and other nations, from the aboriginal people of our islands in the middle of the Pacific Ocean. We share a similar history of losing our traditional lands. We also share a similar commitment to regaining and perpetuating our culture."

My scrawly notes look to me like someone else wrote them. But I know the voice I hear is mine. "One hundred years ago our political and cultural sovereignty was stolen by a small group of foreign sugar planters backed by the United States military. Now we fight to regain that sovereignty. Part of our mission is to restore our cultural and spiritual tie with the Earth, a tie similar to that of all Native peoples. We work for a time when once again we will regard all the Earth as sacred, when we do not distinguish church buildings as the only holy places.

"One hundred and fifty years ago our king gave us the words that are now the state motto: Ua mau ke ea o ka 'aina i ka pono. The life of the land shall flourish when all is set to rights."

I hand back the microphone, stand beside the MC. The drums resume. And out of the dancers comes the young man in black and white. He takes my hand, holds onto it, locks his eyes into mine. "I shall always remember your words," he says. "Thank you."

The announcer thanks me, the elder from the purification ceremony thanks me. Vernon thanks me. I walk away, sit on a wooden box to recover. Again I fight tears. I am proud of myself, a Native person standing among other native people, standing to be counted.

But I must do something with Vernon's tobacco, now sculpted by sweat and shaped by the life line of my hand. I sit on the box, my tobacco hand as useless as if it were in a sling. I cannot throw this gift away. I must honour its sacred meaning. In a few moments it comes to me; I'll wrap the tobacco and take it home, to offer it to Pele, our goddess of the volcano. I'll offer it for all of us trying to keep our heritage alive as we face the turn of another century. To Hawaiians, Pele is the literal, fiery force that destroys the old land and builds the new. To me she also is the symbol of my people's metamorphosis, and of mine, as we rise from the shards of our shattered culture. From Pele's ever-dynamic work is formed the earth.

I fetch a paper towel from the ladies' room, carefully wrap the tobacco in it, and walk down the path that leads out of Fort William along the wide and gentle Kaministikwia River, down the path that leads from this land of strong and gentle warriors to my homeland in the middle of the Western sea.

the child standing alone sings
(a residential school history lesson)

there was time
when children were sent away.
there was a time
when children were sent far away.

there they learned many things:
not to speak their language,
not to listen to their ancestors
not to respect their culture,
not to listen to their grandparents;
not to pray to their spirit,
not to listen to their own "self".
there they learned many things.

some returned, some couldn't.

they, each one, was like
a child standing alone
between
two parents
fighting.

the children had children
of their own,
but remain as
the child standing alone,
not knowing how to give
all the things they were
not given.

today,
the children, today's generation
are returning
home seeking the elders

who remained.

let the children
lead the way back;
teach them to sing the songs.

and
let the child standing
alone sing too the songs,
and
let the child discover
a healing song.

Story-teller

i want to
reach into the heart of the old stories,
and feel the beat of the drum
around the former fires of my ancestors.
and when the story-teller steps out to speak
i want to hear the words
as they were meant to be said:
the lessons, the humour, the
accompanying gesture, the rhythm,
the connection created with the
community, the families.
i want to hear the words
come alive as the fire burns
into the night.
i want the words
to enter my body
and when i speak
the stories to come alive
with today's ears, eyes and spirit.

becoming woman

and there was me small and wordless
struggling to impose my presence
even as i melted to the ground beneath my toes
and the wind carried my voice to the tops of the maple trees
left it hovering in nests afraid to fly
afraid that trying would leave me wounded
when the ground pulled me down yet again
but wanting to taste the clouds
wanting to be seen by those other ground dwellers
as free and brave and beautiful as i dreamed i could be

and there was me tripping and skinning my knees
wanting to be unbending
sure as the escarpment behind me
but losing the battle not to cry instead
wiping pebbles and dirt from the scrapes
while the others jumped from the cherry tree
the blossoms floating around them like magic
i watched while my face burned
saw them for a moment suspended
using their own power to push beyond the force of gravity

and there was me always a step behind
or left forgotten in my hiding place when the game ended
and the others went home to eat their soup and fry bread

and there was me keeping my secrets quiet
waiting to be discovered
but emerging hours later to no one
nothing but the pangs of hunger that keep memory alive

and there was me growing and realizing the dreaming had
begun
that i could stop fighting my shadow
and move to the edges where the centre of my world would set

spinning
the thoughts that would give me the freedom of swallows
wings

and there was me kneeling at the shore
seeing myself for the first time
as i cupped my hands and reached

                    the water was cold against my teeth
                              pure to the touch
        i gulped the water and wiped it across my eyes nose mouth ears
                    then i knew for certain who i was
                    and in that moment i could speak

            i was alive

Mind's Eye

Noreen had been drinking heavily each weekend. She thought it either luck or irony her working at a major chain of yuppie-hippie coffee shops. Here she had a wide choice of a variety of coffee to ease the hangovers. Thank god she had a prescription for T3's to take on Sundays because she'd probably be crazy or even dead by now.

A regular at the coffee shop had asked her out and thinking it would be a nice diversion from her usual weekend binge, Noreen agreed. The movie they went to see was written and directed by a child actor now grown up. Noreen always remembered him bare-foot in overalls and the show's theme music would play in her head. Now he was a successful Hollywood movie director.

The movie was a love story about an Irish couple immigrating to America. Noreen and her date sat in the darkness and enjoyed their popcorn and pop and the movie. Halfway into the film a scene of the Oklahoma Land Rush appeared on the gigantic screen. There they were! Settlers! All lined up in their wagons and horses and ready to go. And like a children's party game, they were off! The prizes were chunks of Native land.

Noreen felt a King Kong size hand slap her across the face. She couldn't believe this little child actor she had watched grow up and she had grown to admire would actually glorify something she really hated. Noreen couldn't believe this yuppie-hippie guy beside her, who probably thought they could have a cross-cultural love affair, actually brought her to this movie glorifying something she really hated.

In an instant Noreen was out of her seat and running down the aisle to the screen. She jumped up on the stage and yelled out to the audience, "You people think this is great? Well, it's not! It's wrong. What's wrong with this picture? This is wrong!" Noreen pointed to the screen.

The projected picture cast Noreen in a surreal glow making her a small distortion in the lower centre of the film. Noreen felt like an actor in a vaudeville show and liked the feeling. She continued, "Land grabbing other people's land! Don't you get it? Oh, you got it all right. You got it all!"

"Get the fuck outta the way, idiot!" someone yelled.

"Hey, it's a crazy squaw! Someone shoot 'er!" yelled another.

"I think she's gonna burn those wagons," commented another.

Two ushers proceeded to carry Noreen off the stage and escort her arm in arm back up the aisle to the front exit. Noreen glanced at her date as she passed by and saw him trying to hide under his cute little Guatemalan cap with wisps of blond hair peeking out.

A cop car was waiting in front and in Noreen's mind the back door magically opened by itself. A crowd gathered to see which star was exiting to this limo. Noreen waved to her fans, "Good night dawlings. Next show at nine."

Noreen sat on the plastic mattress of the lower bunk hugging her bent legs. She rested her head on her knees and stared at the jail floor. She was contemplating how easy it was for a person to let themselves go crazy. If you want it bad enough it could happen. Just let yourself go.

Noreen had always admired crazy people. She would occasionally see them on the street or the bus. The one she took particular notice of always seemed so happy. He was always on the bus she caught to work. He would head straight to the back and lie across the elongated seat. Propping one leg up and crossing the other over he would enjoy the music of his walkman, completely oblivious to all other normal people who would eye him with distaste.

Noreen wanted to be part of that world. She hated this world. She hated this city. She knew everybody thought she was inferior. She could feel it emanating from them. Sometimes alone in her apartment she could feel negative thoughts coming through the walls. The thoughts weren't actual words but she knew out there the general masses took it as a given, "Indians are the lowest." When she went out in the world she could see it in people's eyes. Now she knew the way to get out of the ugly way she felt. She would just leave.

First stop was a memory.

Noreen was twelve when she got a stamp collecting starter kit for Christmas. In the spring she would bike to the neighbourhood library to study stamp catalogues. For a break she would read Tigerbeat magazines and gaze at pictures of Donny Osmond and other teen idols.

On one library visit Noreen started to file her pre-teen nails with the metal nailfile she carried in her pencil case. While contemplating the photograph of one particular teen idol Noreen wondered if she'd grow up and marry someone rich and famous. She started to imagine this scenario and smiled at the idea.

Quickly she was brought back to reality by a tight squeeze to her wrist. "You're going to have to leave," said a stern looking librarian as she snatched the nailfile from Noreen's hand.

"What?" said a confused Noreen.

"I could call the police but as long as you leave and don't return, that'll be good enough," continued the disgruntled woman.

"What did I do?" asked Noreen.

Another voice interjected, "Oh, she's pretending she didn't do it now. Isn't it like them people, lying all the time."

Noreen looked for the first time at a grey-haired woman standing by the next circular table.

"You were threatening me with your knife," resumed the elderly woman in a malicious tone.

Noreen was as equally shocked at the accusation as she was that it was coming out of the mouth of a little old lady. She thought all elders were kind and caring no matter what colour they were.

"I never did. That's my nailfile. I was.." but she was cut off.

"Leave now, or I will call the police," warned the librarian.

A group of library patrons had gathered and Noreen stood up and walked out. She had a hard time riding her bike home through her tears and when she finally made it home Noreen went straight to her room and cried herself into a nap.

"Wakey, wakey! Time to go little lady," a voice echoed through the concrete walls.

Noreen opened her eyes. It was check out time at the crowbar hotel. She pondered the daydream she just had. It was so vivid she tried to shake that woman's voice out of her ears. Noreen knew if she could see that old lady right now she probably would stab her.

Once outside the police station Noreen lit a cigarette and debated whether to go back to work. "I'm probably fired," and with that she decided to go to the bar for a beer. She looked at her watch and knew the bar just opened.

Noreen walked toward the main drag. She looked ahead and spotted an old lady, almost still if you didn't notice the walker in front of her lifting up and moving forward every now and then.

Noreen tried to imagine the woman's thoughts and was looking forward to being face to face with the slow moving target.

Noreen knew she was an innocent good little kid but because of being an Indian other people felt she was less than them. Noreen knew if this woman looked at her the wrong way then she would be forced to say, or do, something not nice. That's what was expected of a downtown Indian.

Noreen was a few feet away from the woman when a dark figure ran by and like a scene out of some action movie knocked the old lady and her walker over then grabbed her purse and ran away.

The old lady turned her head and looked up at Noreen. Noreen looked down at the woman lying on the sidewalk, looked into her pale blue eyes and expected to hear the same cutting voice she heard long ago but never forgot.

"He took my purse," was all she spoke.

Noreen noted the haltingly hurt sound and noticed no trace of cruelty. For a split second two opposing forces waged a one-sided battle somewhere in the back of her mind. Noreen knew it could be circumstance but nevertheless she took off her leather jacket, folded it, placed it gently under the woman's head and shouted out, "Someone call the cops or an ambulance, now, please!"

Noreen sat and waited with the woman until help arrived. The city wind blew dust in their direction and Noreen repositioned herself to block it. No words were spoken between them until the sound of an approaching siren could be heard. "Thank you," the older woman managed to say.

Noreen looked at her again, smiled and said, "That's alright."

I'M AGE

i'm age
image of woman
female of species
enchanting
light of the moon
passion, encounter
vital fluid of life
cosmic clockwork
eternity.

illusive dream
image of woman
short tight skirts
fast cars
twenty foot round
rotating bed
mirrors to prove
mirrors say
that is me
you
us.

image of woman
skeletal
full with child
she stumbles
through a desert
a desperate search
for hope
a bowl of sustenance
plague free water
i hear a voice
from the back
comment on her bare breasts.

REPATRIATE

they dance
stepping to the beat
of Mother's heart
bright colours swirl
bells, cones, jingle.
the midday sun
scorches my eyes
sting in a bitter
yet joyous way.
they dance
for the old ones
for those here and now
and for those to come.
Mother's heart continues
to pound
with ancient footsteps
through times of sorrow
in times of joy.
detached i sit
outside the circle
wondering
what its like
within.
feeling shy
stupid
i should know
what these songs mean.

i feel
incomplete
not knowing
what they say.
the sweat burns me
beautiful names
never given me
colours
out of reach.
i dare not
raise my eyes
not knowing
what to do
what to say
how to smoke
how to pray.

never having
belonged
i know not how.

COLOURS

When I was little
I attended nursery school
down on Broadway and Langside
that's where I'd met my friend
Cheryl.
We were inseparable.

One day after playing with some new kids
I'd come home with a head full of lice
I was sternly told to never play there again
those people were dirty.
I could tell Mom was mad
by the way she scrubbed at my hair.

At daycare, this girl Rosemary
who i didn't like very much
asked me if i knew why Cheryl was black.
I didn't know;
she said Cheryl was black
because she never took a bath.

Later, Cheryl came over
and wanted to play
I knew I wasn't supposed to
not with dirty people
I'd get lice
get heck again.
So I pushed her away,
hard
but she wouldn't go.
Teacher saw us fighting
and took us away
to separate rooms.

A while later,
she returned to say
that I'd hurt Cheryl's feelings
she didn't understand
why I suddenly acted like I hated her.
I said I didn't
it was just that Cheryl was black
and Rosemary said it was because
she never bathed
and I didn't want to get lice again
or I'd get my hair scrubbed hard.

She looked sad and asked,
Do you like flowers?
Yes.
Are they not many beautiful colours?
Yes.
When Creator made the flowers
they were painted many colours
to make each one special.
In this way the people were also painted.
Like Cheryl?
Like Cheryl.
Like Rosemary?
Like you,
like me.

Decisions

Emilie stood at the corner. She had to make a decision: to go to school or go to the restaurant and wait. Emilie's mind was on the man who danced in her dreams each night; the man who made her blood tingle with anticipation. School didn't matter. The only thing that mattered was being alone with him.

• • •

Ten minutes before he started his shift, Sam, the waiter, sipped his coffee. What, he thought, do I do now? What do I do if she comes in? She's only sixteen, yet I really get a charge outta her. I like the way she looks and the way she swings her legs off the stool when she's done her coke. Hmm, I really could make those legs swing. I can't do anything about it though. She's too young, and yet? Maybe later.

• • •

Emilie was sixteen and yearned for the tall waiter with dark wavy hair, and electric blue eyes fringed with thick dark lashes. She craved for his arms to hold her. She wanted his hands to mould her flesh and touch her heart. The ache was unbearable. Emilie no more wanted to be in school than she wanted to be at home babysitting her brother.

Brunette hair hung about her thin shoulders. Her ebony eyes held generations of memories; the pain of her grandmothers as they spoke of the residential school and the education system that had changed their lives; her grandmother's songs of grief as they left their natural teachers behind in their villages. She didn't want to be like her grandmothers sitting in their homes or at bingo with a taste of bitterness on their lips. Emilie knew she wanted the taste of sweetness and she knew where she had to go to fill that desire.

• • •

Sam wasn't interested in waiting on tables, and he wasn't waiting 'till the end of the week for his pay check. He was free, twenty-one and Cree. With twenty bucks in his pocket, he gazed at the door of the diner. He knew in a moment he would leave. He remembered the old men as they sat with their beers in their hands, their stories on their lips and the dim lights flickering in their eyes. That light would go out soon. The spirits were quietly leaving town.

• • •

Emilie set her books in her locker and left. She walked away from the school. School no longer mattered. The halls of polished tile, and the walls of painted wood, were like a prison. Emilie needed light. She needed the spirit and the freedom of youth. And she needed the freedom to fly with her dreams. She strode toward the centre of town. Emilie was no longer a school girl but a woman full of want.

• • •

Sam was ready. He hung up his apron, and donned his Blue Jay's cap. He tilted it a little to the side and pushed it to the back of his head. Sam was ready. Throwing his Wrangler jacket over his shoulder and crooking one finger in the neckline, he ambled to the door. Turning, with his free hand he tapped his finger to his forehead in recognition of his boss, as he opened the door. Just as he did, Emilie's outstretched hand turned the handle and entered. Sam took her hand in his and together they sauntered off.

• • •

Emilie's mind was a flurry of thoughts. Where are we going? What is happening? Are we going away together? Oh God, he must love me too. Would they live together forever in his little apartment? She noticed the palm of her hand in her left coat pocket was sweaty and nervously twitching. Her heart raced. She had imagined all kinds of things laying in her bed alone at night. She had let her hands caress her body and imagined them to be Sam's. Emilie had never been alone with a man before. Her casual friendships with boys were a disappointment every time she came home from a date. She never let them touch her because to her they were mere babies.

• • •

Sam glanced down at Emilie by his side and smiled his sideways grin. This could be a dream he thought. She is so beautiful. Oh man, I could just take her right here on the street. This could also be a nightmare. I know that this could be the best day of my life or it could be . . . what? Is this my ticket to heaven or is it my ticket to jail?

• • •

Emilie followed him, just as naturally as if they were together for the last one hundred years. Oh, this must be where he lives. Is his room here? In the bar? It was at the top of the stairs above the

36

hotel bar. He took her in his arms at the bottom of the stairs and ran his hands in her long hair, twisting it in his fingers and holding her close. Oh God, I'm so happy. Her body trembled as she felt his arms around her.

. . .

Her shampoo smelled clean and fresh like lemons as it mingled with the stale smoke and beer that was floating on the breeze outside the bar. She smells so good, he thought, holding her tightly. Taking the stairs two at time, he ran, hand in hand with Emilie. The tingle of their touch electrified the air as he reached under the mat for the key.

The dimness of the room was unnoticeable in the lights that danced around their bodies. He left the lights off and the bit of light that shone in the windows gave them a clear path to the room. They stopped long enough to remove their shoes as they made their way to the couch. Sam tossed the cushions on the floor and pulled out the thin spring filled mattress. He attempted to straighten the sheets and the one thin blanket crumpled from last nights sleep. Damn, he thought, why didn't I make the bed proper. As Emilie made her way to the bathroom, Sam nonchalantly tossed his shirt to the chair across the room.

She turned the water on in the sink and let it run. The thoughts of him knowing that she was sitting on the toilet made her blush. She took her barrettes from her hair and loosely brushed it back over her shoulders. Thoughts of forever drifted and mingled with the fear that inched its way throughout her body.

Emilie returned to the room. She twisted her barrettes in her right hand. Her fingers of her left hand twisted the curls of her hair which draped down the front of her right breast. Sam took the barrettes, set them on the table and took her in his arms. He held her close to him with his right arm and gently rubbed her back. His hand crept up towards the nape of her neck. His fingers slid down over the curve of her buttocks.

A shiver ran through her as Sam caressed her behind. He nuzzled her hair and placed little kisses on her ear lobes and neck. She's so young he thought and just as quickly let that thought drift from his mind. He helped her remove her blouse and slide her skirt over the gentle curves. Her skin tingled with every feathery kiss.

Emilie in turn let her fingers twine in Sam's hair and stood on her tip toes to reach his full lips. Her fervent kisses, wet and biting, left his lips and trailed down his neck to his chest. She was there with him forever. Nipping his flesh she made her way to his nipples and took them between her lips and drew little circles around each. Sam could no longer stand on his wobbly legs. They fell in each others arms to the battered old couch that was now their chariot.

It was now late afternoon. He thought of her and then his mind flew to his job or the fact that he had walked out on it. What now?, he thought as he reached across Emilie to grab a coke and take a gulp. His palms were sweaty, and his hair all a tangle. Emilie lay among the sheets, her hair tumbled over the pillow, like wisps of dandelion fluff on the wind. Sam looked at her and thought of the eiderdown that covered him as a child, how soft and warm that was. He traced little trails over her arms and along her neck to her breasts. He gently kissed each soft globe and cupped them softly in his hands. His kisses ignited the flame that smouldered inside her and she reached for him again.

Long into the evening they held each other. Gentle caresses mingled with fiery branches; her passion unyielding and his stamina spurred on by the drive to consume all of her. The lights of the night danced across the walls as they made love.

As darkness fell, Sam and Emilie untangled themselves from their euphoria. Heading for the shower Emilie asked herself - what now? She was no longer a school girl. Sam sat, running his fingers through his hair. What was next?

Emilie soaped herself and let the water rush over her head. His shampoo smelled of tar, but she had no choice. Her hair clean and her body tired and sore, she stepped from the shower and looked for a clean towel. He had one towel and it lay in a heap on the floor. She hung it over the shower curtain and thought of fixing the place up. She would buy new towels and maybe some curtains for the windows that overlooked the streets. Emilie put her jeans and shirt on over the damp underclothes, and made her way into the living room.

Sam glanced at her and smiled. He wrapped the sheet around him, tucking it in toga style. He nuzzled her neck as he led her to the door. Sam didn't speak, just kissed her and looked into her eyes before opening the door for her. As she left the room, he locked the door behind her and leaned against it. His stomach plopped to the bottom of his feet. Had he made a mistake? It was too late now.

He had no job, and she was only sixteen. Sam knew the conse-
quences.

• • •

Emilie danced on wings as she made her way down the stairs
and up the street to her home. She didn't think of her mom and dad
until she rounded the corner. She prepared herself for every answer to every question that they might throw at her. At the door her
mother looked at her and hugged her. Emilie felt the twinge, a
small spring coiled and unsprung. She stepped over the threshold
into the next level and never looked back.

• • •

Sam showered and dressed and made his way down the stairs.
He turned at the bottom of the steps and entered the bar. The smell
of stale smoke, and the sourness of spilled beer mixed with the
Dustbane attacked his nostrils. Country music droned from the neon
lit jukebox shoved against the wall. Sam ordered a draft and took a
gulp. The pungent taste couldn't remove the doubt that trickled
down his throat.

After hours of smoke, music and beer, Sam stumbled up the
stairs. He didn't flop on the bed as he had done in the past. He
grabbed his bag and tossed in his one clean change of clothes,
tooth brush, razor and comb. Sam knew he could buy whatever
else he needed in the next town. His trip down the road in a big rig
was his ticket to hauleeewood, and the life of perpetual freedom
that he craved.

• • •

It was dawn. Emilie rose from a troubled sleep and padded to
the bathroom for a shower. She dressed in her school clothes and
made her way down the stairs. Emilie stopped in the kitchen and
grabbed an apple. She wrote a note about some early school activity and left the house. Emilie bounced down the sidewalk towards
town.

Upon reaching the building she ran up the stairs. She took the
key from under the mat as Sam had done the day before. Emilie
entered the dim room on tip toes. She made her way towards the
bed. She felt for Sam. The bed was empty. Emilie stood, and turned
on the light. The bed was just as they had left it. Sam wasn't there.
Gone. The word 'NO' came to her lips along with thoughts of
'fool' and 'love'. Tears flowed down her cheeks to lips that just
yesterday had kissed and nibbled.

She made her way to the stairs. She remembered her mother and the words that she had said over and over again. *No one ever takes anything from you. You are always in charge and you have the choice to give something or not. If you give something away, remember to give it with love. Have no regrets. And always be proud of the gifts that you give.* Though she was a woman in sorrow her thoughts were now on how to succeed. Her determination showed in the sharp, steady steps that carried her to school. She did not want to end up like the grandmothers, sitting at bingo, with bitterness on her lips.

Emilie strolled into the school and went to her locker. She picked up her books and walked in a deliberate step to her first class. This was no longer a prison to contain her. This was a stepping stone to the future. She knew in her heart that somewhere out there Sam was waiting. He just didn't know it yet.

THE DANCE

Through the wind
    across time
Strikingly fast...revealing his strength
    defying Gods angels
Beneath the sea of clouds
    Creeping, reaching, impellingly
Soaring his soul to mine
    Muffled, "I shall have you"
The clouds cloak the sun's energy
    and he has encased his presence inside of me
"The door has been opened"
    What?
Unpleasantly clearer, "The door has opened"
    And beneath it
Spilled out their cries of those who live with-in me
    "Sh...Sh"
"Come now, I am here"
    The train has speeded up
And there are too many crying...calling to me
    I am less now
Parts filtering away
    I plead with them
Come with me
    Sensations of whispers
Caressingly...obsessed
    I flow in silk...of no colour
Turning swirling
    Dancing enticingly
Leaving the ground
    I enter the surge of the alluring presence
The sway of my silken gown connecting
    To the blackness of his cape
Now united
    Our dance has left the Lord behind
Shadows emerging from the cracks in the floor

Others from hell come out of the wall
Their forms materializing
    Floating, dancing, bewitching
In a long ago familiarity
    That I now remember so well
The ache becoming clearer
    The rhythm magnetizing
The door has...been opened!
    Daddy is here
He has brought someone...deeply felt...with him
    My eyes burn from the wetness behind them
Could I walk away?
    They have found the essence
        To divide my soul
One is angry
Sapping it all

A String Around Their Fingers

No open doors
 She tells him lets leave,
Take my hand, remember?
 A broken film repeating
Must detach
 Born of the same
Closer than most
 Twins is what they call them
She sits in
 On the whisper in his blue eye's
Painting the truth
 With lightning's hand
Awakening her soul
 And she knows that he is her right side
With out a sound
 He is alone lost in his subconscious
Unaware that she is with him
 Or is it that he is with her
        A string
        Around
         Their
        Fingers
Shaded from the sun
 Sheltered from their mind
Priorities bubbling
 Striking
One at a time
 Exposing the circle that keeps them dormant
An unprotected
        Obscure
            Intensity
        They must see
            Unitedly
                A time no-longer
                    But with
                    Them

Her Touch

I stand afflicted
       Again
Time passes
       Waiting for know-one
Move the darkness, Lord
Let me feel what I can only deny
       I chase the realities
       Of
       My frame
     Ancient history
I take her existing
       Touch
Intimidated, and running
From what my life is
       Focusing on
Parts of me
       Screaming
         Liar
Spinning shelter
       Colours
That are real
And others?
Each person has their own road, you must find yours
                    Yourself...to be free

Stone

A
House
Of
Stone
And she
Belongs
To
Me
Once again
Calling
Crying
I move in
And
Out
Of
The
House
Of
Stone

Sketchings

Holiday
Can you hear it?
A stream slowly weeping
Its swirl
Tearing at the center
Squeezing the soul
The waters flow is submissive
With composed sketchings
That she has not balanced yet

Always There

The cold has come again...black
And I hear her
She is quieter now, still she is stronger than before
You have a choice and then there is no movement from my heart
Fight...dare...breath
The cold is callous
The black...denyingly raven and there is no movement
And I call on the Lord
Solid, cold and black...it covers my right side
With three arms that entangle my courage
>   Must oppose
>   Or
>   Utter
>   Goodbye

Cherokee Wisdom: Balance the Earth

The very essence of Life is the continual balance between the polarities of the universe. Such polarities include positive and negative, good and evil, love and fear, yin and yang, spirit and matter, day and night, joy and sorrow, dominance and submission----male and female.

These apparent "opposites" are in truth only the two halves that make one whole, this whole being the total experience of life. They do not, as they appear, work against each other, but in fact complement each other. If you doubt this, try connecting only the positive wire to your electric lamp and see if the light comes on. Or, even more important, what would be the future of our race if all the men returned to Mars (where a current best-selling book says they are from)----or just women went to Venus?

Any attempt to avoid the struggle for balance leads to nothingness; it is the balance of these dual polarities that brings about the harmony of the universe.

The Cherokee Woman at the time of the discovery of The Americas had more rights and privileges than the married woman of Turtle Island today. Women not only owned the property, participated in both the fighting of Wars and the Councils of War, but also sat with the Civil Councils of Peace. Lineage was traced through her Clan. Upon marriage, the new husband was expected to live with the Clan of his wife. To get a divorce, the wife simply put the husband's personal belongings outside the door of the lodge. There were no legal entanglements over the division of property or the custody of children, for all the property of any value already belonged to her, and the children belonged to her Clan. The husband belonged to another Clan; he wasn't even a blood relation!

This was not the "petticoat government" that some enterprising journalist dubbed it in those times; it was a balanced male/female culture where each one knew his/her privileges and responsibilities, and where equality of the sexes did not mean that they were cloned copies of each other.

Then along came the White Man with his Great White Father Paternalism and reduced the Cherokee Woman to the passive role of procreation. For the White Woman of that time was in the position of a submissive, economically deprived wife, under the aggressive dictatorship of her husband.

The imbalance in the male and female roles came into being with the shift from rural-tribal to urban-mechanized living conditions in the Old World some centuries ago. It represented a moving away from the feminine characteristics of nature, spirit, mystery and the arts; and toward the masculine characteristics of war, power, material possessions and mechanization.

Women of today have come a long way toward their rightful place in the sun, but have not yet reached the position of the Cherokee Woman at The Time of Discovery.

Astrologers tell us we have arrived at the Age of Aquarius; the Metaphysicists say that the Harmonic Convergence ushered in a new and enlightened era; the Hopi Indian calendar indicates that the Fourth World is nearing the shift into the Fifth World; the ancient Aztec Calendar reveals that the Fifth World is near its conclusion and the Sixth World is imminent. Cherokees say the Fourth or Fifth World count makes no never mind nohow, for time is cyclical and the Worlds follow each other around the circle in perpetuity (that's forever).

Psychics such as Ruth Montgomery and the late Edgar Cayce predict a global upset before the turn of the century. Even the woman in the street can plainly see that Women's Rights are progressing upward and onward, so far in a somewhat bloodless revolution.

It is to be hoped that any or all of these changes will be on a consciousness plane instead of physical cataclysm. And that the Women's Movement does not mean that women are merely taking on the characteristics of men, but that they will bring the male/female polarity into balance.

Road Allowance

The bulldozers came with angry voices
shouting for old bones to lay silent
absolutely still. By this time
the living had been relocated
toe tapping and fiddle music
replaced by the crunch of gravel
beneath steel-toed workboots.
So you were patient.

Now the job is done. The new highway paved
flat and black as the night
and silence has made you
restless. As occasional cars pass unaware
green fingers push cracks into the certainty
reaching toward the hum of tires
the breathing of sleeping children
the weary conversation of travellers.

My Lodge

This will be my lodge
skin stretched tight over bone.
This I will call my home
sacred place I cannot leave.
No light visits me here
the darkness thick
with hot, stone-breath.
Moonlight beats
in the ear of the world.
Stars wonder
where I have gone.
Trees lean listening.
My soft voice centered
rises and falls
with the wind.

Native Reality #2
(for Nora Chapa Mendoza)

Dear Coahuilteca Elder,
woman of spirit and wisdom,

With the sincere hope that Pachamama continue to protect and provide for you, with wishes for peace, good health and lightness of heart, I send you these words.

The traditional altar we erected at Casa De Unidad in Detroit for Dia De Los Muertos (Day of the Dead) celebration was criticized by an 'art expert' from the other culture. He said the red metallic paper we used was out of place next to the natural and found objects of the altar. He acted as though it was his culture that was being misrepresented. I tried to explain to him, Nora, that the metallic paper reflects light better than paint and how we could not paint the floor in front of the altar where the red paper lay. I explained to him that paper (and paint) is the solid material form through which symbolism passes on its way to gaining power and expression. Everything used in the altar comes from the same earth that gave them all birth. Red is a colour that can assume diverse forms and textures. The Red Road Path of our ancestors, which is what the red paper represented, often narrows to the point of disappearing and becoming invisible to the naked eye, yet it remains as witness to the truth of the red sun and blood that course through our veins.

The 'art critic' did not understand how we were forced to accept, borrow or liberate the symbols of the oppressor in defence of our way of life, our homes and our people. Often we wore the enemies clothing and personal belongings to take their power and absorb it into our own to make ourselves strong. We took their foreign religion and gave it our own shape. We transformed many of their symbols from negative cycles into positive life-giving protection. We continue to believe in a Great Mystery that is beyond human description.

We agreed to construct the altar in order to reclaim the Indian holiday and to honour our deceased relatives and friends. It was done in solemn acceptance of death as an integral part of life, free from morbid fear, yet respectful of deaths immense power. We teach our children not to fear the inevitable but rather to prepare for it by living a good life. I wonder if our critic friend was disappointed not to find human fingers and hearts piled on the altar mantel. Maybe we should have asked him to sacrifice himself for the sake of art and his concept of reality.

Maestra Nora, we are descendants from the same humble Nahua mountain culture of the Chichimeca north. We originate from the same soil shared by the Lipan Apache, Yaqui, Karankawa and Coahuilteca religions of the Sun, simple and beautiful beyond description. Our Indio-Mexican Moon into being. Ollin is the invisible glue that binds all things to one another. Our kin are the Villistas, Farm workers, Chicanos and Spaniards. Our extended family reaches far to the north and south of this wondrous Indian continent.

We have seen and done much. Many words have passed between us and we have known one another a long time. Although separated by many miles in distance our thoughts meshed and choice of colours matched so easily to bring the altar to life. I look forward to seeing you again soon. It was an honour to have worked and shared with you. Please accept this humble writing and a handful of Tobacco given with deep respect and thankfulness.

New Mexico

Quarter moon
with her back
turned to the wind.

Dine silver gleams
on black velvet.
Santa Fe
Indian market.

Shiprock leans into the wind
a ghost
before the Spanish Main
and galleons filled with pirates
and priests with hearts as hard
as gold.

Grandma Begay
tours the bars
kerchief frail
turquoise on her arms
"Do you wanna buy some silver?"

Dust devils dance
the never ending song of change
sand scattered and arranged
in bands
red, grey and brown
the healing
whorl of time.

Tonina

"Love is spontaneous firing
of two spirits simultaneously engaged
in the autonomous act of growing up"
- Durrell

Sitting alone
in the Bytown theatre
shoulders
hunching in
I sink into my seat
arms gathered like wings
pulling all the edges,
the rough parts in,
smooth surface to the world
eyebrows furrowed
lips compressed
I realize
I'm
mimicking your stance
and in a second
unconscious becomes caught
struggling
in spider cords
stretched tight.

I feel at
any moment
Satori
might come
kicking down
my door.

veil of timelessness

if
if I could lift
the delicate veil
and step in time
with timelessness
i would
but i am i
and you

feel the wall
of the labyrinth
with hands with eyes that fear suspect
seek the distance

laced in sleep

yes
if i could
i would
dance barefoot
on the breath of a lady slipper

even become the heartbeat
of a panther
giving
shape
to the darkest
night

yes and
even become the space
'tween the whale and her
element

breathe
breathe deep
yes yes relax
that space
at the top
and at the bottom
of the breath
there yes

come
come lets dance
through the veil
'ts okay 'ts okay 'ts okay

Lysol

You walk by the park bench
bleary eyed

smell of Indian funk

Just like me 'cept
you wear your pain like a badge of honour

It is pain isn't it?

Trying to forget, trying to fit
trying to give a shit

The dance of powwows past

spit running down your chin

The real reason? You want the real reason?

The reason is I won't give in.

Someone told me that our alcoholism
was the longest ongoing protest against colonialization

someone else told me their brother committed suicide

I watched my granny's face
eaten up by cancer

I heard the owl call my name so many times
I went deaf in one ear
or maybe that happened when I fell outside the priest's house
too drunk to catch my fall

Only buffalo I ever saw
was the stuffed head on the pawnshop wall
where I got eleven bucks for my jacket that one winter
(Frank's one of those guys'll go out of his way to help you out of
a bind)

I choose the pain the hurt the snakes on the detox wall
or so I'm told

Everyday I create myself
within my barbed despair

I fan the cinders

Hey where you from?
Hey where you going?
Hey fuck you.

John

Today I thought that one day I would dedicate something to
you, that big story of our lives that I will one day write,
retelling on its pages all the tragic pain and hurt and sorry
we carried around for all those many years.

I thought I'd dedicate my autobiography to you,
that I will one day write
chronicling between the covers
the too much shit and pain I've waded through
and the gift of healing I've found in these later years
(and how sorry I am that I can't know you now,
when I should be better able to hold your hurt and pain)

I thought I'd place on the first page of the book

Dedicated to the memory of John Karl

or

To John

or

Dedicated to the memory of my brother.

I don't know when it'll get written but I want you to know that I
will have written chapters on you

on all you are to me,
of all we shared together
and all we should have shared together
and the lasting mark you left on my life

My 11 months younger brother

gone
forever

A young man with dreams and hopes
A young man faced with enormous obstacles
because...
just because...

A young man who found the shouldered responsibility of

just being so enormous
that at times it broke your heart
into so many pieces that eventually you couldn't mend it.

I thought I'd say somewhere in the margin

how I would have burned sweetgrass with you

and smudged you when you felt lost to yourself
and folded you in my arms and prayed for you from deep within
me

I'd mention the hurt and pain of being a child from an abused
home you carried through your life

How jail became a right of passage
(we all came to share)

Passage
into
powerlessness
and
not realizing

why
we

were

(powerless that is)

I would mention how I would like to have you here
to hold and cry and hold you and cry and hold you and
never
let you go away again

I didn't realize your pain was so deep
that time we went on that three day drunk to Calgary

I thought you were stronger than that
I thought it fit into a bigger picture for you like it did for me

When I spoke at your funeral all those words about being
someplace better now,
somehow freer
I meant it

I do believe that you went away to prepare a way for me
so I wouldn't be scared when its my turn
or when those we love
are gone but
I still want you back.

The Blackbird Cage

There is a cage in a sunlit room. A bird sleeps. A songless bird. In a cage covered with cotton.

The cage is round. There is no beginning, no end. This cage is a trap. This cage is a door. A trapdoor to freedom. Freedom wriggles and spirals and stretches like a child, for that is its nature.

In another room, breath is drawn. In this other room, dreams come fast and easy to those who sleep. The dreams are of rocks and shells, feathers and tongues, skies and wings. They are of the long ago and the yet to come. They are of bones and seed, icicles and leaves, the spirit moon, heart-berry moon and a bear standing in the late snows of spring.

The silence will end when the dreamer awakes and the cage is opened.

I was sitting at my desk making plans to visit my sister and her newborn son when the phone rang.

'Hi, Keesic.' There was no lilt in her voice, just a simple statement of acknowledgement.

'What's wrong?' My sister never called me by my full name unless she had something serious to discuss. And since we joked the most when all was well, serious tended not to be good.

'What's wrong?' more frantic now, fear gathering in a lump in the throat.

'Ma said I should call.' She paused briefly. 'Gran had another heart attack.'

There was a long pause, neither of us wanting the words to make our fears true.

'She's dying.'

The trip was a blur. No thoughts, no images are retrievable. Except me. One before the trip began. Except for the moment before leaving when I stood across from Robby, my supervisor. And the image of her face hangs clearly in my mind. A round face, blanching slightly, brown eyes floating, then lips moving. And thin sound of her voice, struggling to escape from its throat, cracking notes of assent.

Running through the halls of the hospital six hours later. Finding no one. Awash in a strange silence. Dread, unacknowledged, growing inside. Moving down corridors. Finally, my sister's room. And my father sitting by the window reading the newspaper.

I stood staring in his direction and he looked from behind the paper, snapping and folding it in his lap.

'I can't find anyone. I can't find...'

'They're at Aunt Lila's. Mom too.'

'But... Gran?' knowing the answer but refusing to believe it, ignoring what I knew and asking the question with an odd innocence.

'She's gone.' Just that, 'she's gone' and picking up the paper. Just that and I am left standing, clutched in the steel grip of a monstrous grief, unable to move legs or arms or eyes or mouth. Just standing immobile, tears splashing through gravity, like a salty river moving of its own accord down the banks of my face.

'Go look for Darlene. Go look for your sister.' His arms still holding the newspaper.

I move instinctively, moving across surfaces, between walls, without thinking. As if a wire had become disconnected. I saw but didn't recognize. Doors, walls, signs, elevators, nurses, people carrying flowers and pushing I.V.'s down corridors. My feet knew where to walk and somewhere in my brain the signs were deciphered. Somehow I did not slam into walls or walk over people or trip on my own feet. But I could not have named one thing, not one item or one letter. I could not have looked down and thought "foot" or "shoe". I saw and moved on instinct, not understanding.

And there I was at the glass window where the newborn are displayed.

Darlene came walking out the door from the room where the babies are fed. I turned to her, arms hanging as if my hands were weights, and she put her arm around my shoulder and walked me back to her room.

I had seen the latter stages of dying though I'd never witnessed death itself. My great Aunt Kayla sprang straight up in bed, her mouth opening and closing uncontrollably, eyes wide open seeing nothing in the room. And I knew I would never see her again.

The experience was poignant and brief and in some unaccountable way, natural and life affirming. My father's death was long and numbing. He never trusted doctors, hated blood, they found the cancer. Too late. Within two months he was a witness of who he had been. He was in and out of hospital. His hair fell out and eventually he was unable to walk upstairs unassisted. With all the desperation of medical science, they hacked him apart and we watched him disappear bit by bit. He spent the days and nights on a borrowed hospital bed in the living room. His temper, which had never been good, became a seesaw of saintliness and rage. Then, after one particularly painfilled and irksome evening, he suffered a stroke and the left side of his face slipped loose. After that he refused to look at himself in a mirror. Saliva gathered and dripped from the left side of his mouth and his words were limp and slid together into a series of grunts and groans. He rarely slept. When he did, he dreamed of birds clawing their way out of his chest and he'd wake up screaming and moaning. In fits of frustration and anger, he began hurling anything within reach at anyone within range. That practise stopped soon enough though, when the pain worsened and we had to give him morphine to keep him from screaming night day.

When he died I was in town buying groceries. When I returned, Darlene, Aunt Lila and Mom were seated around his bed. Mom was holding his hand and an air of peaceful calm suffused the place. And I felt, I knew without asking, that the pain and suffering had ended for everyone in the room.

Dad's eyes had been closed and, laying there surrounded by family, he looked relaxed and strangely healthy. I realized then how the pain had stretched a mask of disease across his face and, now that it was lifted, how terrible and solemn it had been. His spirit had attained freedom and in that freedom had shaken loose the body. Without the spirit, the body ceased struggling. Without struggle, the mask came unhinged and disappeared. As I stood touching my mother's shoulder it occurred to me that the illness had been overcome after all: he was free at last.

Gerry is the only man I've ever loved.

We met at a dinner at his parents' home one early spring evening. His mother had become a fast friend after coming to my aid at a poetry reading. Two Greedy Minds had been circling, quizzing me about life on the reserve, Native spirituality, the appropriation of Native stories, land claims the rights of sportsfishermen versus Native fishing right... I tried, politely at first, to extricate myself. Then I exuded an intense disinterest that bordered on deafness. I openly daydreamed. Imagined myself becoming birdwoman, darting and circling to freedom. To no avail. One persistent, bright eyed university student continued asking about sweatlodges and potlatches while regaling me with stories of her various brushes with spirituality. All with the kind of open faced wonder that could drive a pacifist to throw punches. She stared, hanging on my every word and gesture. My hand was a clenched fist. Barking in my other ear like a dog chasing his own tail, was a plain, fifty something man with a greying beard and balding head. Like all the worst ones, he started out chatting about this and that "Indian" friend of his before launching a tirade about tax breaks and gun wielding warriors.

Caught between the two, I was about to step back and knock their heads together, very hard, when a woman grabbed me by the elbow, saying very sweetly as she hurried me towards the door, 'we'd like to say it's been a pleasure...but it hasn't.'

We left, politely nodding and smiling right and left.

Outside, we walked without talking. The air was as cold as knives in our lungs and we slowed, pulling our scarves over our mouths. At the street light, she turned to me. 'I'm Joan. Hi.'

'Hi.'

'Tough room.'

'No worse than most, I guess.'

'Scary thought!' We laughed together and I knew then that we would be friends. We spent the next three hours in a diner, drinking tea and talking about our work. Joan was also a writer, also Anishnawbe, and on a book tour for her latest novel. I should have been both embarrassed for not recognizing her and humbled that she had come to my reading. But, oddly, I felt neither embarrassed nor humbled. I felt at ease, as if we had been friends for a lifetime and there was no need for such an undercurrent of pride.

Gerry came to the dinner late, with a young, slightly drunk woman hanging on his arm. He grinned and shook my hand warmly, reciting a couple of lines from one of my poems as he did so. We chatted amicably for a few minutes before the meal was served and shortly afterward he and his friend shouted their goodbyes from the foyer and left, laughing and slamming the door behind.

I bumped into him several times during my visit, always shar-

ing a smile and small talk. A kind of friendly disinterest character-
ized all of these meetings.

When I was a child of seven or eight, I found a blackbird in-
jured at the foot of the glass doors of Gran's sleeping cabin. And I
borrowed Grannie's old bird cage and placed the bird inside. Within
a few hours the bird was sitting up, looking around curiously. But
I was afraid he hadn't fully recovered. I was afraid to release him
in the dark, on such a cool night. Instead, I put a margarine dish of
water and some sunflower seeds inside and covered the cage with
a piece of white cotton. Then I went to bed happily, dreaming about
how Bird would sing in the morning. And when he was completely
healed, I would release him. Oh, how he would circle around my
head in thankfulness, how he would dip and dive in his unfettered
joy at being saved. And though he was free, Bird would stay with
me from then on. He would sit on my bedroom windowsill, chat-
tering secrets in birdtalk.

Early the next morning, as sun streamed through the window, I
anxiously lifted the cotton. Bird's dead eyes stared up at me from
the bottom of the shining chrome cage.

Gerry has the eyes the colour of a late winter afternoon sky. A
deep vibrant blue-black, warm and penetrating. My German father
had blue eyes but they were implacable, like pools of cold water.
And he could hide his emotion easily beneath their cool surface.
Gerry's eyes were filled with shadows and valleys, fierce storms
and gentle rain, midnight skies and the soft hues of dawn. When I
looked into their changing colours, it was as if I could see everything he was thinking and feeling. And the first time I kissed him,
it was his eyes that had drawn me in.

And from that moment, I fell into him with abandon.

A room, pale yellow and shining. Rows of sunlight through
slats reflect on chrome. There is a disturbing lack of depth. Everything is flat, white, bright, antiseptic.

There is another room within the room. A place where dreams
have space. A place for real living.

Whispers leak around the pale yellow room. Hissing, shifting,
shuffling, Bodies under bright with cotton. There is no screaming
that can be heard.

Our coming together was like glancing up and seeing a sky
filled with falling stars. In a dark room with the tea kettle bubbling, we touch unexpectedly, accidentally almost. And there was

a moment when our eyes widened. As if to say, who are we? Who is this 'we' that two people become, who this 'us?' And I looked into his eyes and I kissed him full on the mouth, swallowing his words. Then tongues meeting, probing, loving, a new language was born. A language like all language and unlike any other, unlike any we had ever known. Tongues pressed against teeth, lips against lips, creating the sound of this language, the lilt and pattern of it, the glottals and sibilance. Together, with the kettle steaming and shouting behind us, we became the grammar and expression of this language. And through us punctuation and diction arose. A lexicon was created. And spirit pervaded the language.

Gerry gave me gifts collected on the beach down the road from his mother's home. Every night I would find a shell, a stone, a feather on my pillow and every morning I would awaken with new eyes, new ears, and a full heart. So it was that meaning was conveyed and understood and gained depth.

And his mother was a quiet observer to what we were becoming. Without intention, she became the ears to our mouths and tongues, the listener who realized the sound. Without her, it is possible we might have slipped into another world, the world of dreams and spirits, and forgotten our way back to the threshold. We might have slipped and never found life in this world of earth and sky. This world where babies suckle their mothers' breasts and the forest hums the energy between the trees. This world of our waking existence.

A screaming bird battering itself against gleaming bars. A black bird crying in a cage of bloody, hacked off beaks.

I am sitting in the living room of our home. Gerry enters, cold and sweating. Before I can speak he collapses at my feet.

Since I have seen his eyes, through a mask of pain, struggling to give expression to this thing. To find words for what can not yet be understood. Since then I have held him through long nights in strange cold rooms. And held his head, stroking his sweat slicked hair, as he retched and shivered.

Sitting on plastic chairs, I have waited, I have waited. I have listened to the odd echo of heels clicking on tile, my ankles absorbing the coldness. I have seen images of bone. Images of heart and breath and stone. I have watched an image of heart and breath, rising and falling, rising and falling. The heartbeat an unsettling beep and silence, beep and silence. I have surrendered my dreams to a thin green line.

Between visits to this cold bright place, we lived happily. But as this thing grew and Gerry weakened, a terror intensified. And the time between folded back on itself. Then the cold place became home and home, the visiting place.

There is a figure of a man. A silhouette on snow. Snow and sun and a solitary man stumbling.

Snow blindness. Eyes burn and water. Brightness blinding whiteness. Snow and sun and a solitary man stumbling.

The barrens. No beginning, no end in sight. A circle of white. Snow and sun and a solitary man stumbling.

I could not bear to look in Gerry's eyes then. Could not bear it in the yellow room where more and more days and nights were spent. Could not bear it in the living room. Could not bear it in the bedroom. For the first time, I began to close my eyes when we kissed. And a silence rooted itself in our tongue.

So for a time, a space grew and it was you and I, he and I again. And a new mask was fashioned for each. Gerry's mask was a thin transparency that exposed and highlighted his eyes and mouth. Mine covered my eyes and ears. This is how we might have continued in freezing, quiet desperation.

Then one day, Gerry fell on the hard, white tile, knocking the masks loose. And in that instant I saw a blackbird stand in the corner of his eye.

There is a child, waiting to be born. And Gerry and I weep together, our hands encircling my already swollen belly. We have remembered our reason for being and the tears are a language all their own. Translation is inept.

When our tears have said all that can be said, I whisper to Gerry in the language we have come to speak fluently. His eyes are beautiful oratory of understanding. Now, again, Joan is our ears. Now, she has become paper on which our words are written.

As prayers are recited, family gathers. So the ceremony begins and ends and continues in a circle of language.

I open the cage door.

This story is dedicated with love to all free birds, especially Rangi Chadwick.

Alteration

The Rise & Fall Everlasting

1

Coyoti ran all through this one, I can tell
He stopped here left his mark there
Trotted, Coyoti speed that is, over to here
he may have laid down for a while there
His marks are all over this place.

2

What wasn't said during last nites skirmish
was that the words fired back and forth
in blind artistic fury were fully loaded.
Each ballistic babble carrying a payload of armour piercing
syllables with megatons of force.
How any soul could walk away from such a
verbling inferno defies logic.

3

The piercing gaze of emotion drips thickly from your eyes,
I only feel the heat of your emotion,
only can answer each furied thrust with one of my own,
The boil of two bodies so intense with finding
the core of each other only pales in the desire
of your eyes.

4

He didn't have to bring the salmon back for the people,
Coyoti, that is.
He didn't have to free the children from Owl woman
and I wonder why he tricked mosquito into tearing
himself into those millions of harmless bites.
Just imagine the enormity of Coyoti's steps.

5

A whisper a sigh a light brushing of lips to skin,
the glint of tooth polished smile a shiver of
uncertainty at the height of loving. The rise
& fall everlasting.

6

I wonder if Coyoti came because of love
or love because of Coyoti.
He was here though cause he left his marks.

About Leukaemia
for Ellen & Jeremiah

She reaches into the little boy's body
deep inside she reaches deep into the pain and finds joy
she reaches deeply into the past
she reaches for the joys of the healthy places
she reaches for the joys of love
the joys of love she reaches

Coyoti must have made a mistake here too
maybe he fell asleep again in that place
but fox will wake him up soon
That's okay if the blood is tainted because
he left that part with her
and she reaches deeply inside the boy
for life... for love.
Coyoti knows...

Pieces of Glass Resembling a Human Heart

Blue Reservation mornings,

I am recovered by sobbing explosions—whiny country chords
of Garth Brooks which Cousin Cookie has detonated in the living-
room.
She keeps the volume at maximum while she pieces together
star-quilts

or restores rodeo-dud-fabric in her yellow sewing room down the
hall.
An expert seamstress, she handiworks the prom gowns for the
female student body at Popular High. She draws her own patterns,
designs

her own rhythms. You could give her any page from the formal
section in the Sears Catalogue and she'd sew it by heart. Her mind's
eye is a charmed needle—her slim fingers remnants of stained satin
or silk.

Blue Reservation nights

Alice Bought-Plenty arrives to the house delivering years of
regret.
Her shoulders sag from balancing buckets of accumulated tears.
Her mother's tears, her grandmother's tears, her sister's tears,

her own tears. Her broken heart is a country and western ballad
ripped, mangled and torn beyond recognition. She throws the shards
at Cookie's feet.
Cookie gathers the fragments patiently, tenderly, as if she's collecting fragile

and valuable pieces of glass. Alice stands waiting at the door while
Cookie repairs her damaged heart. With surgical grace Cookie
bastes the brittle splinters using her own regretful years as a guide.
She stitches Alice's heart with ancient

strands of her grandmother's hair. The needles she uses are slivers
of her children's bones. She knots the ends of the threads with
mercy, with blood. The vessels are secure, the chambers sealed.
Pain cannot arrive if it hasn't a place to sleep.

1-900-Deliver Me

* * *

Glenda, my psychic friend from the psychic friend
hotline delivers a message
in cryptic detail--
a tree falls in the forest,
a woman in Iowa stirs lime flavored jello,
a schoolboy in France eggs a nun,
a thunderstorm breaks out in the Himalayas--
Three dollars a minute and all I get is static interference.

* * *

Browsing the yellow pages I came across a delivery service that
promises redemption. I order a life to go with pepperoni, olives
and a happy ending. It's been well over twenty years, and I'm still
waiting.

* * *

The only thing I'm sure of is that I'm not sure of anything.
--Anything else?
Yes, someday you will probably die.
--Is that just another empty promise?
I'm not sure.

* * *

My life is an excerpt from *Waiting for Godot: only more surreal
and more vague.*

* * *

If you empty your mind, they will come.
Who will come?
If you open your heart, they will come.
Who will come?
If you forgive your enemies, they will come.
Who will come?
Please deposit a pint of blood and stay on the line.

* * *

The TV evangelist suggested I cleanse my soul, but I accidently
used too much bleach and now I have no hope of ever recovering
from it.

* * *

I placed an ad in the personal columns.
Wanted: Spirit Animal--
Coyote responded, said he was everything
I'd ever wanted and possibly more--
but later he confessed he was afraid
of making commitments.
Every animal I've ever known has been a trickster.
* * *

If I wanted I could walk the Red Road: only I keep getting hung up in traffic.
* * *

The medicine man told me that my totem was an eagle. You could say I purchased an Eagle Vision, fully loaded in 36 EZ installments.
* * *

"I found salvation in Thunderbird wine." The drunk at the pier
tells me.
"I woke up and saw the face of an angel." The nameless woman
cried.
"I looked to the grey grey sky and Christ was crying!" Mavis
June testified.
Is it possible to be blinded by a vision?
* * *

Sitting Bull was a Taurus. Custer was a Cancer. Glenda my psychic friend informs me that this is essentially the reason they didn't get along.
* * *

Shirley McLaine answered my fan letter. I asked why it was that when the spirits appear to me, they are always laughing? She wrote back, that they were probably watching the re-runs of my life. How can I make them stop? I asked. Did you try switching channels?
* * *

At the annual powwow at Daybreak Star
I purchased a dream catcher from
Wasicu Indian Jewelry.
Minding the directions I hung
it over my bed
and have had nightmares
ever since.
* * *

Someone told me they bought a Plymouth Sundance. I asked why they hadn't purchased a Buick Baptism or a Ford Communion instead.

* * *

I wanted to write a letter to Galileo, only the Post Office refused to deliver it. But somehow I think he got the message because the next time I looked into the night's sky, I noticed the Big Dipper was shaped like a question mark.

* * *

Define irony in twenty words or less:
Irony is when an ice-princess and a proud Indian nation both carry on, in spite of wounded knees.

* * *

As the legend goes, Joan of Arc and Brown Weasel Woman both received visions from spirits to dress as men and prove themselves as warriors. The tragic difference, one found death in battle and the other was burned alive.

* * *

I couldn't make the monthly payments, so my Eagle Vision was repossessed.

Ode to the Horse Powered Engine

"If one were only an Indian, instantly alert, and on a racing horse, leaning against the wind, kept on quivering jerkily over the quivering ground, until one shed one's spurs, for there needed no spurs, threw away the reins, for there needed no reins, and hardly saw that the land before one was a smoothly shorn heath when horse's neck and head would be already gone."---The Wish to be a Red Indian, Franz Kafka

1.
Before chrome pistons, crank shafts and cruise control,
there were stallions, palominos and pintos.
Before asphalt, carpool lanes and expressways,
there were open plains, prairies and sage bowl landscapes.
Somebody's vision of power was ignited--
a new mode of transport was bred,
and a future designed by genius was born.

2.
We used to live next door to a junkyard
guarded by a German shepard named Puppet.
It was strewn with the motor innards of dead cars,
a trash heap of failed metal organs and stale
powerless dreams. On the other side
of us was a field of horses. They stood
all day grazing on buttercups, meadow grass
and the crab apples fallen from nearby trees.
Beauty raced with them. Their bodies were
the carved muscle of a god's extravagant whim,
magnificent packaged flesh of a vision gone to pasture.

3.
I'd like to believe that the plains Indians
invented horses. That those herds of sprinting
hooves were created by the medicine
of some warrior's nightmare-- some

holy man's vision of tomorrow. I'd also
like to believe in Pegasus and Unicorns.

4.

I once dreamed of travelling with a caravan
of mystic gypsies. They didn't own fingers,
but two-forked appendages for hands.
They loved gold, red wine and laughter.
They created fire from their supply of magic
crystals. Nights found them in a furious whirl
of dancing and singing. Their wagons
were pulled by a stock of proud centaurs.
One was fair with the face of a Roman
statue. Another was fiery black
with African features. After everyone
went to sleep--I stole them.

5.

Last March I purchased a car.
The auto dealer wore thick gold
chains and grinned at me with broken
and missing teeth. He sold discarded
engines, snake oil and firewater.
Revving the motor of a Dodge Colt
I heard the roar of 800 horses
trafficking across dust and ash
arriving to the other side of eternity.
"Got a lot of power, this one!"
he promoted. Next he showed
me a Ford Mustang. Except the engine
refused to turn over. All I could hear
was the echo of drums beating against
the generator. Finally I drove home
in an Escort Pony. We bartered
and made a good trade. The engine
still runs, but I could have had something
more powerful-- I could have had a V-8.

6.

Driving to the Park and Ride
on weekday mornings, I am greeted
by herds of horse powered engines
grazing on asphalt in the parking lot.
One morning I find that the herd has vanished,
and are replaced with Zulu trucks
and Masai sports sedans.
On the 6:00 news a coalition
of outraged consumers and civil
rights activist are suing
the auto industry. They win.
I don't know if I should laugh or cry.

7.

Some nights I am shaken
to consciousness by
turning dust. Hoof
prints lie scattered
across my bed--
the now bare room
of my vision
reveals ghosts of equestrian
soldiers decorated
in sashes of scarlet
and helmets of frozen blue wind.
Their words are electric
forcing my will to surrender
from this nightmare.
Some dreams you never wake up from.

8.

Some saying used to go--
you are what you eat.
Now I hear--
you are what you drive.
How will I explain to my future children,
the definition of irony?

9.
The Monster Truck Rally
is coming to the King Dome.
That same weekend,
the gay rodeo is happening
in Enumclaw. Queers on steers--
the poster read.
I can't decide which to attend,
so I stay home and watch
the 6:00 news. They're
broadcasting a story about crowds
of demonstrators and animal
rights activists opposing the gay rodeo.
One guy complains on camera
that the oppressed are oppressing.
Nobody is picketing the King Dome.

10.
On the Ponderosa, Little Joe
gets in a skirmish with some
horse thieves. Hoss and Adam
throw their two fists in the squabble,
the thieves go to jail and the show
has a happy ending. I switch
channels just in time to watch
Starsky and Hutch apprehend
a gangster for organized grand theft auto.
The show has a happy ending.
I'm still waiting for a happy ending.

'Life Long Learning'

An age-old saying that has been on my mind a lot is "Life begins at forty". Why? Because I AM forty, going on forty-one.

When I think back on my life, I'd be considered a 'late-bloomer'. In June 1995 I will be graduating, along with ten others, from an intensive three-and-a-half year teaching program with a Bachelor of General Studies degree. Seventeen years after completing high school!

When I graduated from high school, I just turned twenty-three. My classmates thought I was seventeen going on eighteen! I quit school four years prior because I was failing Algebra 12 and had no definite plans for the future.

After two years of University I still did not know what career to pursue. At the age of twenty-five I got married and gave birth to a son and later, a daughter. I worked as a short-order cook, a chambermaid, program coordinator for a drop-in centre, a hostel cook and many years in the fish canneries before getting back into the educational field.

I always wish that I was brought up in our traditional society where children started learning at a very young age. They listened to the Elder's stories and watched the older children. Throughout their lives, they were guided cautiously and counselled wisely. As young adults, they knew what their responsibilities and purpose in life were.

Today I am almost at the height of my career. I am learning how to speak my parent's tongue; I am a drummer, singer, and dancer in a traditional dance group and soon I will be teaching in an elementary classroom!

As a First Nations educator, it is now my responsibility to encourage youngsters in their life-long learning process. In our modern and multicultural society, all learners merit respect and proper accommodation in the school environment. Children with learning disabilities, special needs, the gifted and the average student need to be enticed with a variety of teaching strategies.

The curriculum has been meaningful and inspirational. The unique history and culture of the aboriginal inhabitants has to be made known. All learners should be aware of the laws, practices, customs, obligations and responsibilities that govern the lives of the First Nations people. Keys to survival are consensus, the maintenance of territories and the organization of the people. This knowledge and the newly-acquired skills will provide a sound basis for learning in all other subject areas and of other diverse cultures.

Success is when your students are proud of themselves, of their accomplishments and are applying their skills outside the classroom. With the help of the Elders and the community at large, the school environment will be an important stepping stone to a fulfilling life.

Assimilation or Acculturation?

I've been thinking about the changes that I have gone through while living in this city for the past thirty-seven years. My parents moved from the village so that we could attend the city schools. We were one of very few First nations families that lived permanently in this city in the late 1950's. While we were growing up, my parents did not speak the language or share their cultural traditions.

I remember very little of elementary school. One bad experience that stands out in my mind was when the grade four teacher yanked me out of my desk because I couldn't answer his question. The only time that I felt really good was in grade six. I did a bit of research on the Iroquois Nation in eastern Canada. The teacher liked my report and asked me to share it with the class.

My brothers and sisters seemed to just drift through the elementary system. Out of our family of ten, only four completed high school. Two of us pursued post-secondary education.

A couple of years of university study seemed irrelevant and a waste of my time. After nine years of marriage and working at a variety of menial jobs, I went back to school.

First I took a job re-entry program. Then I enrolled in a Business Management course. Finally, I was accepted into the Simon Fraser University First Nations Language Teacher Education Program.

During that three-and-one-half years of study, I learned more of my cultural background than I had in my whole life. Today I am a functional speaker of the Sm'algyax dialect; a singer, dancer and drummer with a Kitkatla dance group and will soon be teaching in an elementary classroom! I do a lot of research and am always looking for exciting teaching strategies to share with the children.

For thirty-five years of my life I was assimilated into the non-Native society. I knew and cared very little about my parents' mother tongue and cultural backgrounds. As education became relevant to me, I grew very excited about learning the languages and traditions of my people.

I see that I was deeply affected by the dominant society. As a First Nations educator, I will turn the acculturation process around by learning as much as I can about First Nations cultures and implementing this curriculum into the school district. The unique history and the diverse cultural backgrounds of the aboriginal inhabitants of this territory will be shared and experienced.

This goal is attainable because many First Nations people live permanently in this city; almost fifty percent of the students in this school district are of First Nations ancestry and it is a requirement of the Language Education Policy from the Ministry of Education.

'Why wa'h!...which means "The time is right".

city slick her

one thing
that scared
me as a child
were spirits
i knew i
was safe
surrounded
by concrete
because spirits
didn't care
to visit
the city
and i felt
secure under
my blankets
but now that
i'm grown
it's those
same spirits
that keep me
away from
the city

scene in a supermarket

I wait for a prescription
from the modern day medicine man
and gaze at the thousands of
remedies for everyday ailments
lining the shelves

I see you come
around the corner aisle
An old Native man
pushing a shopping cart
with six potatoes
in a plastic bag

I watch you go
around the other corner
and I have an overwhelming
urge to get up
and hug you
and tell you

I love you
Elder Native man
your humility is as honest
as six potatoes
in a plastic bag

We're both the same
people lost in fluorescent
hunting grounds
Would you think
I was drunk or stoned
if I spoke what I felt
or would you understand?

So all I do is
sit and let this
warm sea wave engulf me
and I notice
I feel better already

The Heart's Of Womyn

Speaking from the heart now,
I must recognize the womyn and children everywhere,
Who have become the target of Canadian Government Policy,
Surviving for the day a part of our everyday struggle,
in a world structured on corporate greed,
They have poisoned our waters, leaving our children with
scabs all over their fragile bodies,
Creating a miserable society which our children question.
As they are not able to see their pain is not their mistake.
A constant reminder to us of the continued battle for the
generations ahead of us and behind.
Speaking from our hearts we'll become strong,
listening to the pains of our children.
Healing our minds of colonial oppression,
connecting nation to nation.
Protecting our children,
defeating the enemy.
Together we are healing.
The hearts of womyn,
The way of our grandmothers,
Born of the earth,
The Trees, Sky, Water and Animals.
Our Mother The Earth The One Who Takes care Of Us.

Dawne Starfire

Born for Strength
for Beauty and Light...
Born to hold Dreams
in the Silence of Night...
Born for Truth
and born to give Love...
Born to Know Always
the Peace of the Dove...
Born for Fire
and Visions Unseen...
Born with a Wisdom
that surpasses all need...
Born for Power
through Spiritual Rebirth...
Born with a Song
that belongs to the Earth...
Born as a Dancer
who answered the Call...
The Great Dance is Life
and she dances for All...

The Wind

I am the wind
that moves through
your being...

Sometimes... A whirlwind...
in constant motion...
always touching
your soul...
but something you cannot hold
or contain...
Sometimes...a hurricane
that tears at
your feelings...
challenging
your beliefs...
bruising you with
the force
of it's being...

Sometimes... a soft breeze
that moves across
the meadows
of your mind...
lifting and changing
the shape
of your thoughts...

you long yet for "stillness"..
while the purpose
and the strength
of the wind
is in movement...

I cannot be
this thing that you ask...
for the spirit of the wind
is in "motion"...
and stillness
is its death...

Turn Of The Earth

you look at me, but don't ask questions
take me for who i am at the moment
        not prying deeper
        not seeking answers
to questions you avoid
hesitant to ask, you are shy
a man who's been to war
and have renounced its evil
you live today
as if tomorrow will always be waiting

taking your time, and not demanding changes
you understand that change happens
        with every turn of the earth
        every wind that blows
        every flicker of candlelight
revolution is a natural occurrence
flowing from the sea, thru the earth
a volcano of change
        shaking all cities
challenging our acceptance of unhappiness and destruction
and asking of us generosity
        in a time of greed.

Spirit People

i've seen your fires burning
and felt your flames
i've witnessed your anger
i've seen it attack children, women
chasing us into the dark, the trees
away from your guns and greed
into the dark, where it's safe
and the coyotes keep watch for strangers

i've seen your anger
and felt your flames rising
i've witnessed your anger
      searing & spreading
threatening me when i'm asleep
unaware of the danger that waits for me & my people

threatening-
but i won't let your torches threaten me
i won't let you threaten my people
we have a place here
a meaning here
a reason to be

we relate a message of hope
and send out a message of love
      understanding
compassion & peace
like flowers in spring
      we search for the sun
opening & welcoming change
not allowing in anger & war
hate that harbours only hurt
hate that harbours only more hate
anxious to suffocate & suppress our spirit

spirit people we are
and within us lives life
breathes life
radiates life & love
giving life to the memory of those who came before us
and the spirit of those yet to come
from seven generations of blood and bone still with us
to seven generations of young ones, rising & rising & rising
spirit people we are

Dialogue About Them

Check them out! What do you suppose we ought to do about them?

Who?

The New Age crazies.

Why should we do anything about them?

Well as an Indian person, don't you get offended by them?

Not really. I see them as really trying to be better people.

Yeah I suppose. I guess they probably have some unmet spiritual needs, but I think they mostly have a lot of gall.

Yeah?

Yeah, I mean, Santa Fe is loaded with crazies. This is the place where some cross eyed white woman listed Shaman as her occupation on the cover of Times Magazine...I wanna know how much for Shaman school and who accredits it.

So you think Native people have the market on spirituality eh?

No. Not even close, which is precisely my point. Why do they have to steal Native people ceremonies in order to be spiritual. It really gets to me.

What do you find that is so offensive?

Oh, stuff like they'll be talking in their melodramatic voice about how 'the spirits' came to visit them on their $1,000-week-end-spiritual-adventure with a woman named Clara Clearwater or something. You know like every time they talk about the Creator they say 'Takashala' and they look at you like you're supposed to have this mutually deep identification and understanding. Like they spoke the secret code word and now the Native people are supposed to let them in the club. I feel bad for the Lakotas and Dakotas and whoever else addresses their Creator as Takashala. To have all these weirdos trying to get in on what they perceive as the REAL spiritual ride to the heavens. You know, like they caught the Native Bus to happy hunting grounds. It bothers me cause, I'm Dine, Cochiti and Zuni not Lakota. It's like they're assuming all Indians are the same and we're not. I don't know much about other peoples ceremonies and their relationships with the Spirit world. It's not my place. There is stuff I couldn't ever know. And I don't think that I would even want to know.

Why not? I mean if you had a chance to see/know the truth, why wouldn't you want to know?

It's just that I don't think that because I get invited to another Peoples' ceremony that I have any rights to incorporate it into—more like onto my side. It belongs to a people. It's their truth.

Isn't Truth the same for everyone? Why wouldn't Truth be Truth to everyone?

It should be, but it's not. There is always different perceptions of the same truth. For example, we mostly can agree that entire tribes were killed off and children were taken away from their homes and made to speak another language, but they forget how recent this took place. Like just because it doesn't seem so recent to them that we should all get over it and move on. I think they forget that millions of Native people died so that these ceremonies could continue. They don't even seem to care about the bitterness that our peoples still suffer from. They're oblivious to the reasons we still have that pain.

Well, I don't think that they don't care; it's probably that they just don't know. We need to inform them. But it seems to me that you're getting bent out of shape is sort of based on your personal baggage. I mean first of all, don't you believe that everyone is a spiritual being?

Of course-

So are you saying that because the Newagers are lacking a cultural place and history they should not try to have their own ceremonies?

All I'm saying is that they have no right to steal others ceremonies cause they've misplaced theirs.

I really disagree with you. I think that wanting and needing spirituality is just enough cause for the New Age movement. Our present time and place is that there is a lot of people out there who could use some spiritual guidance and help. They need it, but even more...they want it. I believe that the holy people will help them out and bless them if only for their sincere efforts. It's not fair to say that they've misplaced their ceremonies and so therefore they're out of luck. What does that say about other tribes that have lost their ceremonies? Do we count them off of our official list of Indians?

No we don't. As far as I'm concerned, there is a big difference between newagers and tribes who are struggling to retain their cultures. Native Nations have suffered genocide, theft, rape and thus colonization of our peoples which has profoundly impacted our young people. Yet we have collectively chosen to continue to believe in our traditional beliefs because we understand this as true. Natural law has dictated the way our people think and live. The cost to continue our beliefs has been tremendous. It's not like we collectively decided that man was smarter and deserved to pervert religion, natural law and disregard the collective rights and dignity of humanity. Many newagers have never accepted that this is the true history and there is a price that the collective has NOW to pay. Personally, I've seen that many of them do not want to deal with the day to day reality of homelessness, poverty and racism. They just want us all to suddenly be friends and pray together. I refuse to pray with people who are not willing to discuss and work against colonization, racism, classism, or the theft of intellectual property. And I'm not saying that they're the racist ones...I'm saying why should they be shocked when our young people say stuff like 'Damn them white trash sure do stink up the sweat lodge. Fucken white trash.'

Yeah, a lot of our people are racist. Which is precisely what I've seen. I've seen many new agers live more true to the traditional ways than even Indian people. They don't litter or drink excessively, and they really try to stay aware of the spirit world. You know racism isn't part of our cultural heritage.

Yeah, I know that. And yeah it's true that a lot of times Newagers are working to live true to traditional ways, but then sometimes I get the feeling that it is a luxury thing for them. I mean, I don't really know the percentages, but compare how many Newagers have to deal with, alcoholism, commodities, poverty in economics as well as education, etc. I don't mean this to be an excuse, it's just a reality that many Indian communities are dealing with. We are having to deal with issues of colonization.

Yeah, well, it's just that I've seen so many of our own young people ignoring our Elders and goofing off in the community meetings. Many of them don't believe in our ceremonies or creation stories anymore.

Well, sometimes that is true. But I believe that this is why we have to protect our cultures and ceremonies. What scares me is that we have been taught to believe that our cultures are trivial and superstitious. The New Age movement hasn't helped change this perception. So many times I've seen the Newagers think that most of our creation stories are to teach little children how to be nice. That our stories are quaint and teach one moral per story. They don't even know that some of these stories are about child abuse, sexual abuse, spousal abuse etc....but that we also have solution-ceremony. The ancestors taught us how to heal our people according to the local means available. For instance according to Dine stories, Coyote is a holy person. He is beautiful, and he can be backward. He is the first one to commit child abuse, yet he is still a holy person. Because he found the way back to health and therefore has given his people a chance for life again. In other cultures it is different animals that serve this role.

I'll tell you a true story. One time this one medicine man agreed to help a group of New Age people thru a bad time. In the ceremony, he was announcing which spirits had chosen to come and help. Well, one of the spirits was the clowns, who do everything backward. He said "They've decided not to come in and bless this house. They don't want to help and they are not going to help." Well, everyone started to cry and say stuff like "I wish the clowns would come and help. I wish they would see to it that they might bless us and this house. We need them here to make us smile and laugh." I was dying not to laugh. And I never tried to explain to them that they were crying for nothing. If they wanted to have a Bozo the Clown experience, then so be it. They were trying to equate their own 'clown' experience into Native communities. They assumed the history and place of the clowns and were really upset. It's their problem.

But if they have no history or place what should they do? Where should they go? How should they come to a place where they can be? Most of these people you are talking about are genuinely good people. They love their children, and animals and this is how it should be. They really want to help and to be helped. I mean, there are a lot of them out there that follow the Buddhist way of life. It seems to really help them. I don't see very many Buddhist people upset over more people following their way of life. They seem to welcome it. And it hasn't destroyed the Buddhists.

To be honest, I don't know a whole lot about the Buddhist People--if they are a people according to the following definition (People is a body of persons sharing a common religion, culture, language, territory, political structures.) I'm not sure. But just going on the way you phrased it...Buddhism is a way of life says to me that it offers principles on how to live life. I know a little about Buddhism, but I don't think Buddhist people have ever considered Buddhism a Religion or culture. Do they?

I don't know.

I don't know either. But as far as Indigenous Peoples go, we are a

People. Some have more of the culture intact than others. We had to fight, plead, work, beg and die for it to continue. So how do the Newagers even justify using the word Takashala—not knowing the geography, customs, language and vision of the people. How?

I believe it's justified in them really trying hard to understand the spirit world.

Not good enough. No way.

So what is their hope? I mean you tear them apart but where is their Place? They're as much displaced as many of us. It hurts. We know that. So where's their future? Why shouldn't we help? Isn't it part of our responsibility as human beings to help bring understanding to end our crisis?

It's true that we all have a responsibility, and I think that our responsibility has to start with honesty...Honesty and willingness to see and be reality. It goes back to place.

Thought we dogged place. I don't get it.

It's like this. Everyone has a place. It's where they are. Not where they think a free ride awaits them. They need to work on finding their own spirituality by finding their own truth and reality. They need to examine, pray, laugh and work hard and see how they arrive at their spirituality by dealing with reality. It's a process.

For instance, I have this one friend who lives in Oakland, CA. She's a young white woman. She is one of the most spiritual people I've ever met. She doesn't talk about God nor Takashala or whatever. I've never heard her espouse spiritual techniques or religious know-how. But she gives a damn. She works hard and she has the guts to see the world as it is. She is a participating member of her own family and community. She sees injustice and does an excellent job of working and searching for long-term solutions. She understands her talents and so she has chosen to work with young people to raise consciousness about issues such as ceremony, democracy and education. She's a damn good listener, and she tells you the truth. Now that's Spirituality as far as I'm concerned. She hasn't tried to run for cover under a God Shield, but rather has become an active part of the shield and has taken some tough blows. I believe that this is where the holy people have great respect and admiration for her and her courage. They would bless her home, her thinking and her vision. One time I saw her admire the early morning Sun and this gave me hope.

Never Again

Never again
Will they take you from our land
Will they cut your hair and douse your head
And rid you of the bugs that only they could see

Never again
Will they strip you of your identity
And make you one of them -
Like all the rest
And steal your humanity,
Individuality
Spirituality

Never again
I say these words
Watch
As you cut your hair and douse your head in colours
To expel the internal creatures
That only you can see
To erase the pain and grief
That you carry for your parents
Grandparents and ancestors
the endless pain

Once more I hear the words
Never again
As I watch you walk away
To the cities and towns
To the bars and streets
Still carrying the pain
I yearn to bring you home and say
Never again

And yet, look, I am there
Beside you,

Within you,
Surrounding you,
I am there
Haunting you
For I,
in my pain,
Did the same
As our grandmothers and grandfathers
Stood helplessly by
As you were taken
By their ways, their words,

Never again I say
As I walk away
No longer a child in their cities,
In their towns
Their words no longer control
Their liquor no longer runs in my veins
My blood flows red with my ancestors
Pumping, beating the drums of our songs,
Our hearts,
Our spirits
Now soar with eagles, ravens, hawks
And carry our prayers to
Shogwayadishoh - Creator
We will tell our children
And grandchildren for generations
How we have endured, survived and maintained
We say never again.

Eruption

mountains erupt from inside my breast
dark jagged pain explodes
to meet the clear blue of my tears

sharp, razor,
cutting pieces of my flesh

your words,
your hurts,
your slash
across my face
across my back
my tears join together, flowing
ebbing towards my heart
to wash away the debris
to wash all poisons
from my gaping wounds
and yet

you stand before me
unashamed
you dare look upon me
with no regard
for all you do
you walk upon me
as if I were your slave
to be owned and done with
as you please

It is with contempt you
glance,
and tread
and dance upon my breast
you tear
you rip

you shred
to leave a gaping wound
for which there is no mend
that you can ever fix

I leave you now
I will not trouble you again
for I will be fine
without your greed,
your hatred
your fear

I need you no longer
I no longer care
for your abuse

I will be ok
when you are gone

she reading her blanket with her hands

part i: dear diary

jan 28

be patient, my grandmothers tell me.

listen to your body
trance yourself into your body
in there you will feel warm and safe

this woman I know, she calls herself my friend, she pulls her arms
and makes her body like a star. she wants to hug me, her gesture of
friendship. she takes herself back from me and keeps her hands on
my shoulders to make us one. she says, why don't you just face the
truth? you're white. you don't just pass, you're white. you're not
metis, you're white like me. you shouldn't do what you do, she
says. all you do is romanticize and exoticize first nations people.
you're not realistic, you're idealistic.

jan 29

from way up there on the mountain top where the air is thin and
cold and the snow is white and the stars

oh the stars

oh the stars

there is a consciousness of a kind
of vertical relation between the stars and
white male man (and/or
oh white woman)
white male (wo)
man is under the   stars

oh the stars with their white light

their white noise

                                        white
                                          white

white	fire	white
white	fire	white
white	burning	white
white	bright	white
white	I	white
white	wish	white
white	I	white
white	may	white
white	I	white
white	wish	white
white	I	white
white	might	white
white	I	white
white	wish	white
	I	
	white	
	white	
	white	
	white	

this woman I know, she calls herself my friend, she moves her hand across to mine to make the white man's shake, her gesture of friendship. she says she doesn't believe that whites married with indians way back when, maybe nowadays, but not back then. you're white, she says. I've always thought of you as white. how can I look at you any other way? I'm a woman of colour. I experience racism every day, you don't, I won't be your caretaker, you're white. you're not metis, you're white.

jan 30

the word symbol has now gone a little stale; we readily replace it by sign or signification the symbolic consciousness is essentially the rejection of
               form

the paradigmatic consciousness defines
meaning   as a veritable modulation of co-existence, ja?

form: totemism

signifier (the totem) signified (the clan)

white?

white?
write

right

I'm at a pow wow, a toddler crawls my way. she knows I'm special knows my spirit's big for little ones. she climbs my way. she's on my back she's in my lap she's on my back she's in my lap she wants to sit to cuddle to sing to me. she points. her mommy's over there. over here she's crawling back she's on my back she's in my lap her mommy's back she pulls her from my lap. it's okay, I say, I'm a breed I'm not a white. ya right, she says and takes her girl away. her little arms her hands reach out across her mommy's back she starts to cry to cry her mommy's slap, you can't go back you can't go back she's bad she's bad she's white she's white alright?

the syntagmatic consciousness unites
signs on the level of discourse itself

the totem: white snow on mountain peak
the clan: white (wo)man is certainly the syntagmatic consciousness which most readily renounces any (other) signified

the signifier (white snow on mountain peak)
postulates the signified (the clan)
as sovereign, extracted either from an anteriority or
from a history

he's tory, ja?

fade-out: in television, motion

pictures, and radio, a
gradual disappearance
or fading of a sequence
(a section of motion-
picture film
presenting a single
episode, without time lapses or
interruptions)

fade-in: in television, motion
pictures, and radio, a
gradual coming
into visibility or audibility

jan 31

what's in it for the whites to change?
for the government people for the capitalist people
there's money, no?

for others?
not   white   theory
not   white   supremacy
not   white   power
rome wasn't sequenced in a day, ja?

I'm five years old. my mommy's sad she's sad she's mad they push us here they push us there they push us round and round they push us on the ground. they kick they kick they sing a song: two buck fuck, two buck fuck, squaw squaw ya dirty old squaw, squaw squaw ya dirty old squaw, two buck fuck, two buck fuck. I cry I cry I hug my mom I hug my mom, are you okay are you okay? her face goes rage she's red she's red she grabs a stick she hits she hits my legs my arms my face I'm red it's blood I'm full of blood it hurts it hurts. she hits she hits she howls, you're white I'm white you're white I'm white we're white alright?

(fade-in) oh nothing has changed in five hundred years past the single episode, without time lapses or interruptions in television, motion pictures, and radio, all over the world on mountain tops too the snow is melting melting the snow is melting oh (fade-out)

be patient, my grandmothers tell me.

listen to your body
trance yourself into your body
in there you will feel warm and safe

Mary Jane

She came to me
>from the Milky Way.
She came to me
>wrapped in a shawl of light.
She came to me
>and whispered:
"The hands of grief
>also carry grace."

Motion

>Sky
>moving above,
as the salmon rush north against the current.
>Stream
>rushing below,
as the winged ones hurry south past swollen clouds.
>This planet spins
>like a fisheye
>in an undercurrent.

Visual Pun I

Coyote
toppled
off
the
cliff
landed on his head
and
bounced
back
up
again.

(Right before 5.0 earthquake, Coyote must have been listening.)

Visual Pun II

Coyote
ran
up
to
the
top
of
the
mountain
took one look at this world,
spun,
then
quickly
ran
back
down
the
mountain.

Conversion

She Asked Me

Here we go again, the road, endless, redundant roundabout, Vancouver, Calgary, Toronto, Ottawa. and now here in Northern Ontario, no, that's not true, Southern B.C. I arrived...when? That's what happens when you're homeless like my grandmother said all those years ago when I used to visit her on Spadina Street where she'd sought shelter, taken temporary refuge. A stranger in her native land, she once wrote in a poem, and I agreed and brought her more tea wanting to tell her that for us it's called history, the way things are, not choice, certainly not, maybe accident (Is it?). But I didn't have to explain. She already knew what I was about to say and was nodding her head. I'm sure she could read my thoughts because she asked me not to smoke, which I took as a sign.

Into a dream I awake, and the telephone gathers up space and time in its constant ring. I can already hear a woman's voice before I even pick it up. She is asking me when I'm coming home, our conversation suspended in a breath, a pattern of coloured light. Home? I answer not a little amazed she would flash such a word through me. You mean like home and Anishnawbe land, I almost say, but don't because she is weeping like the child she lost to the street, to an executive position in some bank, though to her it is all the same, the damage done. Her mourning song enters and fills me with the last ring of sorrow for all we've done, from the infinitesimal act of stomping out a tobacco butt to the infinite of stomping out a life, all that which has turned her sons and daughters into strangers.

And again I awake to find myself packing to leave yet again. The room a scatter of suitcases and boxes. All I can do is sit for a moment and stare out to the sky and consider this journey. Yesterday (or was it the day before?) I flew through a haze of smog and landed in San Francisco and found I could barely breathe. Today the Okanagan sky is clear, the wind fresh as can be expected. Tomorrow is where my grandmother sits in a room staring at a wall, where my mother lies in a hospital also staring hopelessly. The end of their journey somewhere just beyond their wait. Earlier in the week, in New Mexico, I journeyed to a sacred place and said a prayer and a whirlwind appeared like an answer. Grandmother, Mother, that prayer was for you, for all of us lost to this century, this land turned highway.

A SPELL IN THE RED

And again the rain fell here on the roof,
fell there on the lawn where, tall in their bed,
the tulips shivered, dropping petals red

as an incision, while here in the house
a game went on and on all afternoon,
two of us spelling across and down and

around the kitchen table, trying with
letters, words and rules--like the one against
the use of proper names--trying with points

accountable to balm and dispel thoughts
of operations and stomach pains. What
good could they do that woman or her son

after all? Only when the telephone
rang could my mother ask a friend--Hearing
noises at night and locking doors--is

this what a widow feels like? Only then
could I hear the drop in her voice of names
and words unspelled, could I think her husband,

my dad might fall out of that hospital
bed in town that day, might land much more than
long distance, longer than the rain away.

At every turn that afternoon, a new
word shivered across or down and an old
petal washed to the ground, in clouds, in sun.

Only when that light took the fall too did
the telephone ring once more, did my dad's
voice rise up, spelling the good news out in

telling how the nurse had just again been
by, rearranging his bandages. Then
we could put the game away, drop his name,

know the tall tulips and their splash of hue
--dark and congealing too in the evening
wind drying the lawn--of course were healing.

LINES UPON THE FLOW

Our paddles are deep in conversation with the river. Hear
how they enter it, each stroke questioning the current? And hear
how the stream replies with an eddy or splash, syllables so

obscure, who can be sure they're adding at all to what's been thought
about night? Neither you or I can tell by a push, a pull
in the thick of dark, in the dark of the flow, its quickness or

direction. Will putting up paddles, letting silences come,
move us out beyond discussion, beyond what carries us
along? Will we come to some conclusion in the current? But

some other tongue slips through on an old and liquid idea
and off into song. And we would join in, sing along if we
could, if only we knew the tune or some words in the language.

How the river mocks our desire, breaks up in bubbles of
laughter in our wake, won't ever take us seriously, as long
as we mistake talk for speaking in tongues. Tongues of light, it
says,

tongues both dumb and bright. The ones, it whispers, that push
upriver
through the sounding dark into a night so clear, you're afloat light
years out in space right here along the shore, the moon in your
throats.

Daddy?

"I'm gonna be a daddy!"

A revival choir couldn't sing louder. My heart clapped against my chest like the hands of those attending gospel church. I felt naturally high. I began to sing again in Praise.

"The Lord has answered my prayers!"

Raising my hands to the sky, I blessed the Creator.

My girlfriend stood stunned. Her home pregnancy test showed bright colours of a definite positive sign. Her eyes were glassy, and her jaw was all but on the floor. Tears trickled to her cheek. I was induced closer to reality with every tear that fell. My heart dropped with them. Numerous questions rushed to be first to my lips. My thoughts broke and poured out into words!

"What's wrong?" blurted from my inverted smile. "Are you okay? Are you disappointed? Don't you want the baby?"

I gasped and tried to regroup as my thoughts ran wild. Maybe it's not mine! I shook my head. Don't be silly. Maybe she doesn't want me to be the father! Maybe she'll leave me and I'll never see my child! Or worse, maybe she'll have an abortion! My heart slowed and then it started to beat faster and faster.

I better sit down! I thought and reached for a nearby chair. I shot back up. My mind was out of control. What about school? Better get a job! What about marriage? I shook my head again. Oh no! what am I gonna do?

She hadn't moved and I felt as though I had just raced an "Ironman" marathon. Powerful to start, what a man! Studhorse! Champion baby-maker! And then I grew weary. I felt back pain. Imaginary cramps pointed sharp pangs to my lower stomach. My head spun and I felt ill. Morning sickness no doubt. I sat down and cried tears of joy. Mixed emotions of anxiety and confusion sprayed from my eyes. In my mind, tears turned into tiny sperm. They fertilized everything in sight. Babies developed everywhere. I lifted my hands to my face and covered my eyes. I was losing it. Just as my head was ready to explode I heard her say, "So, are you ready to be a daddy?" It was then, I dropped to the floor assuming the fetal position. I placed my thumb in my mouth as she rocked me to sleep in her arms.

Assa

I hope you can hear me.

This may be the last time I walk

onto this hill to talk to you.

This sacred ground that holds your bones in silence

is under siege.

The oil companies

want to dig you up and build a road.

Asyoo and I hitch-hiked into town

to stop them.

I tried to translate for Asyoo but

they wouldn't respect a kids voice.

They shoved us out steel doors.

My leg and fingers got caught

and my skin ripped.

I bled on their steps.

Asyoo,

she spit black scuff on their white walls.

Asyoo tells me

her sister, mother, and brother

are here with you.

Why don't they understand

this is our territory.

The Muskeg people's land.

The site where your haaa songs echo.

I have never seen you but

your prophecies and medicine songs

swirl in my head.

Asyoo and Amma say you were the last Nache.

I'm proud to be from this bloodline.

We sang your horse song

the one given to you by the spirits.

Did you hear the agony in our voices?

Assa,

where do we go?

What do we do?

Assa,

please help us

I hear their machines coming

down the hill.

Copy Cats

Black magic

hides in the grass
lost from the night before
Young fingers grasp the neck
and guzzle the sweet black syrup
Little sister and I tell
silly stories of kindergarten
and giggle at our mischief

Black out!

I give little sister the bottle
and set her on the bed
I claw railing and sprawl
to the floor
I slur a drunken scream
help me up

Caught!

This five year old
gurgles to mom
I'm only doing what I've
seen you do
many times before
I'm proud to say
I too have found
the magic in the
Vanilla Extract

Lysol

stands innocently on the shelf
green blue and white
Toxic power hidden.

Flames jump Be careful!
Death lurks inside.
Fancy words say what you are
but they don't tell how often
you have tricked our people to their graves.

These people with the schooling
They read the directions
To disinfect hold upright
15 to 20 cm from surface and spray.
Spray two to three times until surface is wet.
Prevents mildew and mould.
Eliminates odours.

The Indian reads
To get drunk hold upright.
Spray into cup
until you get enough to drink.
Mix with water if you can't afford wine.
Kills bitter memories when used regularly
Eliminates Indianess.

A Summer Ending

Five year old Melanie woke up to the strong smell of coffee and to the sounds of crackling firewood as it burned in the old stove. Its warmth soon spread around the small tent. The coziness of the warm tent made Melanie want to drift back to sleep. She knew it was only five o'clock. Her father Philip always made coffee that time of the morning.

Sensing she was awake, her dog a young pup, came pouncing on her; Mee-quinn tried to lick Melanie's face. Melanie managed to duck under cover of her sleeping bag but Mee-quinn was already sitting on top her and licking her hands until Philip gently but firmly, in a whispering voice said, "Mee-quinn, maa-gee-echez!" The pup obediently walked away and sat himself at the entrance of the tent.

As Philip went out to get some more wood for the stove, the coolness of the early September morning air crept up into the tent sending a chill down Melanie's neck. She snuggled up into a ball underneath the blanket to keep warm. Her mother Sarah was still sleeping in the right hand corner of the tent. A feeling of loneliness and sadness suddenly overcame Melanie while she lay there as she remembered the events of the past week. A young white man with an interpreter had come to discuss Melanie's education.

The small grey car which drove up the dirt road leading to the village swayed to and fro as if it were on a windy sea. The driver, Peter Smith, from Montreal was riding with Mary Cooper, a native of the tiny community of Meqlon. They would be working together in the task of registering students for the fall.

"So, has the place changed since last year, Mary?"

"No, but the Chief managed to get the community centre open for young people to spend their time more constructively."

"That will be a tremendous help for them".

"Yes, I hope so".

As Peter and Mary got out of the car, children began to gather around them and ask questions.

"Mister", they chided shyly.

"What is your name? Where do you come from?"

Meanwhile, Peter was busy trying to avoid the large dog that was approaching him, sniffing his jacket. In Mary's fluent Cree, she shooed the dog walked away.

Inside Philip and Sarah's cabin, Philip was busy carving wood to make a snowshoe, Sarah was making a fresh pot of tea, while Susan and Melanie were engrossed in putting a puzzle together. Just then there was a knock on the door. Sarah was greeted by Mary, the interpreter and a tall, blond young man, Peter Smith.

After they shook hands the four adults sat down with cups of hot tea to discuss the girls' schooling.

Peter turned to Susan who was sitting on the bed with Melanie, and asked her if she was ready to go back to school. Susan smiling shyly, replied, "yes". Meanwhile, Melanie pretended to play with her doll trying to avoid this "stranger" who had come to their home. Peter started to talk to Melanie in a strange language. She eyed her sister nervously. Susan spoke to her in Cree. "He is asking you if you are ready to start school." Melanie nodded a yes and ran over to her mother. Peter entered the children's names onto his ledger and explained that the children would be leaving on September the 3rd, 1969. He then asked for the signatures of Philip and Sarah. Philip slowly wrote his name in Cree on the piece of paper. Sarah did the same. Mary got up, patted Melanie on her head, and smiled. Peter asked Mary to thank Sarah for the tea and not to worry about Melanie. There would be people at the school who would take care of her. With that, the two visitors were gone.

To Melanie's five year old mind, the idea of going away was a frightening thought. She had no idea whatsoever as to why she would have to leave her parents. Nor did she know what she would do once she got there. She didn't understand why her parents could let her go. Her older sister Susan had tried to make her feel better by telling her that she would be there for her.

Melanie's last thought before she drifted off to sleep was that she didn't want to leave her pup, Mee-quinn behind. The pup, now a year and half had been given to her by grandpa Joseph on Melanie's fourth birthday. Just this past summer Melanie had gone swimming at the dock near their home with Susan and Mee-quinn. Susan had taken the pup onto the shallow water and coaxed it gently to swim. Melanie had burst out laughing as they watched the pup swim to shore, shake himself, and roll on the grass. He barked as he stood watching the two girls swim around, then with a leap he was in the water again with them. She had run home that day to tell mama what happened.

When Melanie awoke again at eight-fifteen her mother was busy cooking pancakes native style, thick and crispy. Sarah turned and smiled at Melanie, who was sitting on her sleeping bag wiping her eyes.

"Get dressed, wash, and eat breakfast, my daughter".

Melanie got dressed and went to the outhouse, located further to the left side of the tent. As she came back in she asked; "Mama, where are papa and Mee-quinn?"

"They went to check the fishnet".

Sarah got some lukewarm water ready in a basin for Melanie to wash her face and hands in.

After breakfast, while Sarah busied herself tidying up the make-shift beds, Melanie went out to play on the swing which her father had made a thick rope with a small piece of plywood for the seat. Both ends were tied securely to two trees that stood side by side about two feet from each other. All around the swing the ground had been cleared of any rocks, tree stumps, trunks, branches and sticks for her safety.

The sun was higher in the blue skies, and it was much warmer now than it had been that morning. Every now and then a bluebird flew to peck on bits of fish left on the poles Sarah used to hang the fish to dry. Underneath the poles, which hung in a horizontal line, black embers lay from a fire now long burnt out.

Suddenly, Mee-quinn came bouncing up the path which led to the dock where Philip kept his canoe. With a yelp, Mee-quinn tried to jump on to Melanie as she swung back and forth on her swing. Melanie cried with glee as she struggled to break free from the pup's playful leaps. She jumped off the swing and together they ran off toward the lakeshore to meet her father. Philip was busy unloading the large basin filled with the damp net and wiggling fish.

"How is my little girl this morning?"

"Okay, Papa, did you catch lots of fish?"

"Yes, I did, Melanie".

She squealed as she waved her hands to keep the playful pup from pouncing up on her. They walked back to the campsite with Philip carrying the heavy load of fish on his shoulder. For those few happy moments, Melanie had forgotten about the sadness she had felt that morning. The happy moments spent with Mee-quinn was all she lived for in her innocent mind. These simple pleasures shared by her pup had erased the fear of the unknown which she had experienced in the wee hours of the morning.

While Melanie ran off to play with Mee-quinn not far behind,

Sarah and Philip busied themselves setting up the firewood needed for the fire to smoke the fish after they had been cleaned. Philip walked over and seated himself on a tree stump beside Sarah who was cutting the fish. He took out his pipe, lit it and spoke; "My father has asked me if I would like to go with him to Black Spruce Mountain after the children leave. He wants to go moose hunting."

"Very well, it would give me the chance to start working on those moccasins and mittens. Just make sure that there is plenty of firewood at the cabin before you leave. You know how hard it is to get wood near the village."

"Yes, I will do that".

The next morning at six o'clock the cloudy skies foretold of the coming rain. Outside it was cold and damp, but inside the tent it was once again warm and cozy. Warmed by the wood stove now burning at its peak. Philip coaxed his wife to get up, explaining that they must leave early while the lake was still calm. Sarah reluctantly pulled herself up from the warmth of her blankets and arose to drink the coffee which Philip had made for her.

Melanie was awakened by all the commotion of the morning activities. When she finally got out of her cozy bed, Philip was already taking some stuff to the boat to be loaded and the pup was romping around outside excited by all the activity. After Melanie had washed and eaten, Sarah combed Melanie's long shiny hair, tying it in a pony tail. She gave her a sweater to put on. "Mama, why do we have to go back?" she said sadly.

"Because we have to get you and Susan ready for school."

Sarah wrestled in her mind with the anger she felt at the thought of having her baby taken away by people she had never even met just like they had done to Susan when she had been the same age seven years ago.

On the other hand, she knew in her heart that there wasn't much she could do now. Besides it was for the good of Melanie that she get educated. She hoped that Susan would be there to assist, guide and support her little sister during her first year of adjusting to a new culture. With this thought, Sarah was able to resume her packing and take the belongings down to the boat.

At approximately eight o'clock everything was set and they were ready to go. Melanie eyed the campsite one more time, unaware that this would be the final moment until next summer when she would be able to see it again. She focused her eyes on the swing she had played on as they reeled away into the calmness of the waters with their boat and motor.

The winds, which had picked up during the half hour journey back, were just about to make the boat ride rough when they finally could view the tiny village which rested on the shores of Abitibi Temisgimae. Smoke rose from the chimneys of the cabins, with their brownish tones, that lined the shore. Children's laughter, dog barks rang in the cool air as the boat idled to a stop and landed heavily on the sandy beach. The pup jumped up from the boat and ran off excitedly. Melanie and Sarah went off to meet Susan, who had stayed behind at aunt Mary's place.

A teenage boy, Nick, who was fishing nearby, came by to help Philip unload the stuff and carry it to the cabin. The cabin was cold and empty when Philip first entered it. But about an hour later, the small, one bedroom cabin was warmed by the wood stove, and alive with excitement as the family was about ready for a hearty meal of moose meat stew and bannock. While Susan set the table for six, Sarah cut up the bannock and placed it at the centre of the table. When everyone was seated, Grandpa Joseph recited a prayer of thanks. Everyone started to dig in to satisfy their hunger.

"Susan", Grandma said in a soft voice, "be sure and take good care of Melanie when you get to school".

"Yes, I will, grandma."

Sarah looked at Melanie, "I'm going to miss my baby".

"Yes, we all will, but it is for the good of them that they go", replied grandma Helen.

"True, then my little girl will be able to translate for me whenever we need to go into town".

Joseph replied, "So you will not have to worry if the cashier is giving you the right amount of change".

Helen and Sarah looked at each other and giggled.

"Grandpa!" Melanie's voice rang out, "Mee-quinn ran after a squirrel at the camp, but he didn't catch it. The squirrel ran up a tree".

Grandpa Joseph laughed, "Mee-quinn is still too young to hunt".

The following day Melanie was awakened by Susan's voice. Susan told her she had to get ready to leave for school.

Sunlight coming from the window shone on Melanie's face, she ducked under her blanket to hide from it. Susan playfully nudged Melanie's legs.

"Melanie, it's time to wake up, it's seven o'clock and the bus will be here at nine-thirty".

Melanie, not wanting to get up, curled up into a ball and closed her eyes once more. Knowing what would do the trick to get her up, Susan went out and called for Mee-quinn. Sure enough, the pup went straight to the bed where Melanie slept and pounced on her. Melanie, with a sheepish grin, sat up, and hugged Mee-quinn.

At nine o'clock that September morning everything was done and the girls were just about ready for the bus, which, in a couple of hours, would be taking them miles away from this place they called home. Sarah was fussing over Melanie's hair when they heard a man's voice yell, "The bus is here! It has arrived!" Sarah and Philip looked at each other silently. The day which they had dreaded had come and, with it, hearts heavy with sadness. They both tried to put on a strong face for the sake of Melanie. She was excited about her first ride on the bus.

Sarah, Philip, Joseph and Helen, walked to the bus with Susan and Melanie. A crowd of people, young and old had already gathered at the bus area. They were kissing and hugging one another and shaking hands. While the suit cases were loaded onto a truck, a woman was calling out the students' names as they boarded the bus. Others were crying now as they glanced once more to loved ones among the crowd.

Melanie hugged her pup Mee-quinn, whispering good bye. Choking back tears, Sarah and Philip kissed their daughters goodbye, urging Susan to take care of Melanie.

The fear which manifested itself on the faces of some of the children weighed heavily on the hearts of parents and relatives as they waved farewell. Melanie forced a smile as she waved to her parents and grandparents while the big yellow bus rolled away toward the highway which would take Melanie to a whole new way of living.

A world where the unfamiliarity of a new language and culture would be thrust upon her. Melanie would be coming back a different person. Yet her innocence forbade her even to begin to realize this change that would be taking place.

Her parents knew though, and, as they waved goodbye to the girls that day, they said good-by to the wonderful person they had known for such a short period of time: Melanie, Waa-shaa-shkon, Blue Skies.

Drumbeat

Come here my friend
Sit down and hear
the whispers of our
grandmothers and grandfathers
before us,
What do you hear?
Is it about sadness and
darkness?
or peacefulness and happiness?
can you hear it?
Do you hear the cries?
Of ones who are longing
to feel the sadness
Or do you hear the
joys and sighs
of ones who walked
so proudly and so strong
Who stood so powerful and tall
And can you hear the music?
of drums that beat so loud and so strong
or Can you see it?
The Warriors standing all around you
Greeting you, and Welcoming you
My friend.
Or do you hear
Silence and see
Nothing?

Digs

novel excerpt
from DIGS

Los Angeles, 2030

chapter VI

Stephanie recalled the meetings at which the Hold-Outs had urged the Coalition of Commerce to remove the Mainstreamers from the continent and relocate them in Eurasia. It was their belief that any Mainstreamers left in the new society would plague the continent once again. Just as they had brought with them smallpox infected blankets as gifts for the Natives. Just as they had introduced the drink of alcohol which NPIIC considered the slow smallpox blanket and which had wreaked havoc on Native peoples during the twentieth century. By 1985 85% of the Native population was affected directly by the disease of alcoholism, fetal alcohol syndrome, diabetes, and cirrhosis of the liver. In the late 1900's the esteemed Native actor Dehl Berti had once commented, "T.B., Smallpox, Measles, Alcoholism--they brought all of this with them--the only thing we got of any value in return was eye glasses."

Of course, Northridge officials did not agree with the statements of the more traditional Native peoples. And Stephanie found much use in the modern world for the gifts of germ warfare, nuclear power, genetic code altering, test tube babies, and cloning. She understood their value in gaining control and maintaining power.

The NPIIC had suggested the Euro-Americans be removed from this continent. Northridge was an advocate of a re-education of the Euro-Americans. Of de-programming their combined social consciousness into a state of awareness suitable to the society which had emerged. NPIIC had no clout; Northridge did. Stephanie was proud of her choice in affiliation with the University. She knew they would work for the betterment of mankind, just as the Europeans had attempted to at one time. Though they had failed, she believed they left salvageable methods to attain the goals they had once set for themselves.

Professor Thompson watched her from the doorway, observing her concentration and devotion in her work. She was a skilled member of the assimilation effort and knew what to do. He had taught her all she needed to know. He kept a watch on her for over five minutes before he announced his arrival, as though it had just that moment occurred, "Stephanie, I have returned. Have you enough information to go on?"

She was happy to hear his voice, "Yes. I have more than enough. I am a pack rat, a meticulous note taker, I have enough here to go before the Coalition if need be."

"I do not think that will be necessary." he laughed. "You are something. Good work!"

"Craig," she said and smiled shyly, "I did tell Mr. Stark I was bringing you with me. On the basis of the threats, of course." "Of course," he said, as if he hadn't noticed her using his first name which pleased him a great deal, "We should stop somewhere for a quick lunch on the way over to his home. How about the Burger Hamlet up the street?" he asked.

"I would love to, they have great juice mixes there and wonderful California-style dressings." She began gathering together her compilation.

"Yes, then shall we?" His voice carried the false British intonations so many of those people in prestigious positions utilized. The NPIIC had issued a statement claiming that this was due to the Euro-centricity of the Mainstreamers and was used by endowment organizations as a prerequisite for funding policies. If the representative of an organization applying for funding spoke in that manner, the NPIIC stated, they received funding without the usual delay and investigation or review periods. Many assimilated Native Americans used this technique as well as the Mainstreamers for equal opportunity purposes.

Stephanie filled a briefcase. Thompson carried the rest of her folders under his arm for her. Thompson turned toward the elevators, but Stephanie pointed to the exit sign hanging over the stairwell, "We haven't had any aerobic exercise today."

The descent downward gave her a feeling of exhilaration and she hopped down the last few stairs in a hop. Professor Thompson, Craig, enjoyed her excitement. He felt refreshed when walking with her to her jeep.

As she unlocked the doors for the both of them she said, "Craig, thank you for sticking with me through this. I would have been oblivious without your early warning and help today. Thank you. I am indebted to you." He smiled at her and she felt an inner joy in his approval of her words. They boarded the vehicle and started off toward the eatery.

She avoided the route which passed by the yuppie pub and took an easterly direction off campus instead. Passing through suburbia made her feel as if all of this was worthwhile. She couldn't begin to imagine why some of her fellow Native peoples would want to return to a life without brick homes, without the rewards of the industrial age. She loved the way the tract homes met yard to yard and remembered her visits to the new Santa Fe, that it looked like a modern-day town of Bedrock. Yes, she thought, we must all be the same. It is inevitable and it is right. That is what multi-cultural stands for-sameness. We are living out the prophesy of sameness and conglomeration. She had argued this repeatedly with the Hold-Outs she had encountered in the past. They felt that the indigenous peoples needed time to heal from the centuries of oppression— alone. Stephanie held on to the 90's "New Age" theories of togetherness and harmony. She longed for the day when melanin would be injected into the Euro-Americans in their de-programming campaign and everyone would attain like skin colour. She supposed the African-Americans would utilize a skin lightener to reach the same tone, as well. A former superstar, Michael Jackson, had been accused of this decades ago. The public discovered he actually had a skin disease which lightened his complexion; however, the idea had been born and had been used by others. The African-Americans had been instrumental in the progress of civil rights in her grandmother's days and Grandma had held their accomplishments in high regard.

She thought for awhile about the great discoveries and inventions of the Asian-Americans, the electronic achievements and equipment beyond the dreams of the ancestors. She felt some confusion about Latin-Americans. She was told by her mother that they were a mixed people of Native and European descent, mostly Spanish and Portuguese European, but they often wanted no part of being considered Native. War babies, she thought, just as the

Metis. Maybe it is better that way. She glanced at her own dark skin and thought, sameness solves everything.

Her mother had told her that in the days of the first reservations here, in Mexico and Central America the Native peoples had been convinced to state only their European lineage. There were some Hold-Outs in those areas as well, but they lived an extremely hard life if they chose to remain true to their nationalities. Enslaved by missionaries, tortured, killed for centuries, somewhere along the line some of them broke, as their oppressors knew they would. Many tribes had forgotten their languages altogether. Europeans knew this was vital to a proper conquering. Kill the language, kill the culture.

Stephanie remembered reading in some pamphlets that the Hold-Outs' descendants had compassion for other peoples. They listed an agenda for self-determination for them, too. The Gallah language and dialect were still prevalent in remote areas in lower South Carolina and the NPIIC had suggested a sovereign nation be established in non-native populated areas there for the African-Americans. In addition, they had suggested parts of New York and San Francisco be set aside for Asian-Americans and that some of the very far southwest be laid as an area for the Latin-Americans/Chicanos to have an Atzlan homeland. The agenda addressed long-term goals and permanent lands for these people who were willing to support a Native America, Northern First Nations, Indigenous Mexico and the separate sovereign nations of these tribes and communities within the continent. Stephanie agreed with these plans. She realized that there were some groups of people that could not go back to their homelands, as the Euro-Americans could. Many had not come here on their own free will to begin with, and would not be accepted on return.

Stephanie turned onto Interstate 5 South on their detour and found the freeway full of cars, side by side, of all makes and designs. She took notice that all of the cars contained three or more people. She knew the story of the 90's when almost every vehicle had only one passenger within it. The Car Pool Enforcement Planning, in concept, had ensured less gasoline use, but in reality it had little effect as people would simply load in children that would have stayed home otherwise. She noted this as a target area for change and correction in civil-planning. She secretly hoped to bypass the automotive industry's monopoly on the design for vehicles which ran on solar and other passive energies. It was too soon now. They were only ten years into the program she knew they couldn't accomplish everything in ten years.

Nearing Hollywood Freeway 170, she made ready for a proper turn onto the busy road. She noticed at least one patrol car parked on the shoulders waiting for speeders. That much hadn't changed, it was the end of the month and the quotas were due for the officers to remain on payroll. She adjusted her speed to the legal limit and pulled onto 170 next to a semi loaded with produce from a more environmentally safe growth zone, probably the Amazon meadow which had replaced most of the jungle after the mass destruction of rain forests there. The NPIIC said that if the governments of South America had refused the United States and other dominant countries' actions to destroy rain forests, the aggressors would have been forced to preserve and enhance the lands in North America. Without preservation they would have no farming and ranching alternative. They requested full participation from the governments of South America in stopping this "global war on life and its inhabitants." The newspapers often had articles about the declining life force in the Western Hemisphere as a result of these practices and of the silent and bloody war on the Indigenous in these areas.

Following the lines of cars and trucks, Stephanie made her way to Hollywood Boulevard and exited just in time to narrowly miss a motorcyclist threading traffic on the offside of the shoulder. Crazy, she thought while she checked her rear-view mirror for traces of the biker.

When they reached the burger joint, the professor said, "What is it, Stephanie? You haven't said a word for twenty minutes."

"Nothing is wrong. Just lost in thought, I guess." She stepped forward through the glass doors under the electro-lighting and flash sequence sign. He followed her as if trailing a pipe dream emblem. She asked for a rush to go order since they had little time left for dining.

The waiter hurriedly disappeared behind swinging plexiglass doors soon returning with their order in a recyclable foil bag. The waiter collected their payment and scurried off to attend to others, caught in the hurry of the human race—L.A. style—their heads bobbing in animated conversation, trying to impress and upstage their peers. Stephanie stepped back on the street and jumped into her jeep to make the route to the Starks' home. Thompson followed, jumping in only a second later. Eating while she drove, Stephanie asked, "Could you turn on the radio, please? My hands are full."

"Sure, do you want to discuss anything about the case?" he asked.

"I do want to ask you under what existing clause could they possibly file an injunction to stop the project?"

She took bites between speaking and steering.

"I believe under civil-rights and reburial issues."

"But, those are to protect our rights, not theirs."

She narrowly missed being side-swiped by a small compact car.

He grabbed the handle above the passenger door and answered. "Yes, that is why I believe they will try this to reverse much of our progress."

"Absurd," she said flatly and continued eating.

"You know those Yuppies," said the professor, and he began to eat his meal as well.

They had finished eating when they arrived in front of the red and white brick tract house accommodating the Stark family.

Before leaving the vehicle she reviewed the order of the files with the precision of a mantis preparing to dine. She reorganized the last layer of papers to the mid-section. Pleased with the collation of folders, she said, "We have the upper hand here."

"No doubt," responded the professor and they left the jeep parked along the curb and strolled up the brick walk to the massive house made to resemble styling of the last century.

Knocking upon the door, then impatiently ringing the bell, they waited as Joseph Stark made his way from the kitchen to the entrance way. He opened the peek hole to ensure it was them and allowed them entrance.

"Ms. Red Horse and...."

"Professor C. Thompson," Stephanie offered and extended her hand to him. He denied the sign of friendship as if he thought it less a courtesy than a pandering to authority. He proceeded down the hall summoning them to follow by waving his hand. Stephanie noticed his suit was slightly wrinkled and assumed he had not gotten enough sleep by the rings under his eyes. They coldly displayed every bit of his fifty-two years and then some. His brown hair was neatly combed. Very businesslike, she thought. As they entered the study Joseph's wife called out from the stairwell, "Joseph, do you need me?"

He walked to the stairwell, "Darling, I have this under control." he said. "If I need you, I will call."

Eva liked very much to be needed by her husband. She smiled slightly at him and sharply looked at Red Horse as if hawking her. Eva was relieved her husband referred to her in this way. She felt important and assured he could, in fact, handle the likes of Red Horse and her consort. She knew in her heart that he could handle them, but her mind was troubled. Red Horse, she thought, is another story, a greater adversary. She kept watching Stephanie out of the corner of her eyes until they went into the study.

Stark joined Stephanie and Thompson in the study and found them already seated and appearing very comfortable with the arrangement.

"Ms. Red Horse, I have here some personal belongings attesting to the fact that my mother is the same Ellen Stark whose remains you claim to have found traces of LSD on. I implore you to view this evidence and the paperwork I was able to locate as evidence in contestation of your so-called research project." Stark controlled his emotions as though he were conducting a merger of businesses. This enabled him to be objective and he hoped enabled him to be more convincing in his plea. "Honour is at stake. Our family is of great prestige and has come through much scrutiny over the last few decades with a clean slate. I do not want that slate marred." He looked to her with confidence. As he lay the validations before her as monuments to his mother, his eyes held her complete attention.

Stephanie looked over the pictures asking, "Do you have a diary, or any personal writings by your mother?"

His voice softly lowering, he said, "No, not that I want to be made public. It is my mother, and her personal writings are just that, personal." He watched her to make certain she knew the emphasis he placed on this statement.

"I am only asking for the sake of documentation, you understand." Stark looked at her coldly knowing she would love to read writings on one of her subjects of study, especially one that had drug involvement. He held his ground on revealing any other personal effects at this time, but gave the impression he did possess some.

Stephanie lifted the locket, which was identical to the one Ellen Stark had worn, opened it and found a picture of her in her young adulthood. Seemingly unaffected, she continued on through the pictures. She passed each item to the professor as she completed looking at it. He took care to notice the subtle differences in Stark's appearance--searching for noticeable physical deterioration from drug abuse.

"Is this all you have?" she asked him.

"I have here several papers and clippings from the news during my mother's short life. She was a woman of peace. She wanted no one harmed, only freedom for the people she loved."

Stephanie took out her notebook and began writing notes as he spoke in reference to his mother, while she looked through the papers and clippings he had produced. Undaunted by her documentation of his words he continued, "The Stark family are advocates of peaceful negotiations. We spearheaded many businesses and industries that are vital to the new society and have been of help to your people in initiating the assimilation programs of the past. You have benefited from our knowledge. We are a people who have been displaced, yes, but not outlived and we plan to continue our gifts to society in the new order. We believe we can work with you, but you must stop this insane research on our dead. What can it possibly accomplish?"

"Truth." Stephanie replied. We were at a disadvantage at one time in that we did not understand the value in these research methods, but you convinced us otherwise. We know now it is important to study peoples to understand them. Surely, you agree, after all the years of your research on our people." She watched him through slit eyes pressuring him with unspoken words in the game of subtle interrogation. She was quite adept at duplicating tactics of the Euro-centric teachers in this field of human study; her professors had told her so.

"No, I do not. I know my grandparents were involved in some Anthropological studies in their time, but we are of a new generation. Our people had written pasts you could research on paper and computer discs. He pointed to the computer terminal on his desk and to the dozens of discs laid out in neat rows next to it. There is no need to remove our dead, they cannot tell you anything."

"They tell us more than the living. The findings of the LSD verified the plight of the corporate world in the late 1900's. Their involvement in narcotics led them to fall. We don't want the same mistakes duplicated in our society. This must never occur again. Truth and more progress. That is what the past lives tell us."

Stark handed Stephanie an LA Times picture of his mother leading a protest in 1968. "Look at her, she is standing up for freedom. She is leading the charge. You are taking away her freedom, even in death and violating our rights beyond the grave!" He rose quickly to full height and raised his hand in the air momentarily before placing it over his heart and regaining composure.

Stephanie calmly raised an eyebrow and very quietly said, "Mr. Stark, please, on one is violated. The lab at the University treats all remains with dignity. We do not butcher corpses as did your people. We merely discover hidden facts about the person's life. We document these findings in hopes of making a substantial impact in implementing change for the new world. Since winning the United Reburial issue in the 90's, our people have vowed to rebury the dead as soon as we complete research on the remains, much as the Smithsonian agreed to do way back then with the 30,000 Native remains they held onto for so long." Breaking very slightly she continued, "This, is progress. This, is hope for the future."

Stephanie pulled out papers from within her briefcase and quoted precedents in policy that insured her right to research, based on rights of research the Mainstreamers had taken over the Natives for centuries. She quoted the legislation 'Title 44' for operations such as these, "Due to the Mainstreamers burning all evidence they could collect from the ages previous to the twenty-first century." The evidence had been burned to prohibit the Natives from discovering data they needed to help in their acquisition of power and control. Professor Thompson added in extra information whenever he deemed necessary. He stated that anything historical prior to the year 2010 was mysterious to those who could not remember. The two of them made a remarkable presentation of reason and logic. Stark was unmoved by their legal quotations. Realizing this,

Stephanie resorted to explaining to him the implications of any further accusations against her research.

Calmly and coldly, she began, "Mr. Stark, I regret that this finding has caused you concern; however, it is a factual find, it is a great find. I realize you feel you might suffer some family embarrassment, but the facts are indeed the facts, notwithstanding."

"Ms. Red Horse, I will pursue this until I have put an end to the toll on my family. I will not allow my family to suffer for some ridiculous idea that something can be accomplished by embarrassing people of social stature from my culture. Euro-Americans made this country great."

"Euro-Americans caused this country great grief and raged genocide on The People for a long time." Shaking her head she went on, I see no reason to continue this discussion. You can tune into FOX Television tomorrow for full details on the dig. Is there anything else I can do for you, Mr. Stark?"

"Yes, we are not finished here. I will get my mother's diary. If you insist on making a mockery of her life I will assist you, on the condition you make this person's identity anonymous and retract previous identity as a mistake due to the many graves you are robbing in Forest Lawn."

"Let me see what you have. I am making no promises of conditions until I have had time to view the evidence to decide if it is of any worth to us. I need to weigh the pros and cons."

"If you will excuse me," Stark uttered on the way out, leaving them in the study.

The professor smiled a huge grin at Stephanie, proud at the manner in which she manipulated Stark into producing further traces of the past to them. He knew this could be extremely valuable to the research and when making even a verbal agreement, nothing was guaranteed, no agreement with a Euro-American Mainstreamer was. He mused at the idea Stark had fallen prey to one of the oldest tricks his ancestors utilized.

"Craig, we could find the entire missing components of the family fortune in that journal. I must have it. I must make copies of it for my files. Along with this locket." She took the chain of the locket and held it up to her neck, hoping to wear it as a trophy of conquest. She admired herself in the reflection off the glass on the desk they were seated.

"You do look wonderful in jewellery," the professor said, "you should take more of it, for research, of course."

She watched the glimmer of the metal, pleased at the thought of owning Euro-American traditional jewellery, just as the Mainstreamers had become mesmerized by Native jewellery, for so long. She was filled with the infatuation of being exotic, another race, another breed. She moved the chains slightly to create more bounce of light off the chain from a large crystal chandelier hanging high above. She wanted to be white. She wanted to be European. Stephanie wanted to have privilege, knowledge, to have power The People had never known. She watched the light dancing in her fantasy. Thompson watched the light dancing off her beautiful dark eyes.

woven blue shadows

Your breath is melting
into late night forest wind
urging pine needles
to whisper along the mountain tips

Early this morning I fell outside
my pale blue painted door
into the garden of green leaves
and scattered little bugs chewing pollen

This morning you fell thru my little blue door
a drop of moonlight
shining thru a loosely woven blanket
I wonder where you will create shadows and illumination

Kinship is the Basic Principle of Philosophy

The Thunder-beings are alive:
    grandfathers!
The Earth is alive:
    mother and grandmother!
The trees are alive:
    grandfathers, grandmothers!
The rocks are alive:
    relations of all!
The birds of the air
      the fishes of the sea
      the animals that run
      the smallest bugs
      we are related!

For hundreds of years
    certainly for thousands
Our Native elders
    have taught us
"All My Relations"
    means all living things
    and the entire Universe
"All Our Relations"
    they have said
    time and time again.

And here's the good news!
    The geneticists
    have at last
    learned to read the DNA
    and lo and behold
    they find that the Old American
    elders are spot on!

The white-robes
    priests of the new electric monasteries

have discovered
that animals, bacteria,
plants, trees, humans
all share the same
building blocks of DNA
repeated over and over
in different patterns--
same stuff
just arranged uniquely.

But what a great thing!
to learn that the old
indigenous philosophers
have been right
have seen past differences
have seen through externals
have seen beyond divisions
have penetrated mysteries
to teach us of the
unity of all life--
and without using computers!

But the old wise ones
have talked also
of water
of rocks
of earth
of clouds
of sky
saying:
all my relations
leaving the geneticists
still in the dark!

For DNA does not make life
having DNA does not make
one move
having DNA does not make
one change

having DNA does not make
one "breathe"
having DNA does not make
one grow into a mountain
having DNA does not make
one erupt
having DNA does not make
one unite in congress
with another!

For surely it is that
all of us
have other things
in common
known long before DNA
known long before genes
and I mean
those things,
those structures,
we call chemical elements
like
oxygen
hydrogen
you know the rest.

For surely we already share them
with everything else
we already know we are the same
our bodies have nothing not found
in the earth
in the water
in the air

And the Ancient Ones
already have instructed us
of how
we are one with all these things!

And when hydrogen and oxygen combine
     in a grand sexual orgy
     producing their child water
     do they not act?
     do they not change?
     do they not move?

What could be more alive than water?
     Magic water
     the greater part of us
     alive, are we full of death
     of that which is dead?
No, I won't have it said that
     my innards are dead
     that the salt water core of me
     is not alive
     and all of my acids
     and proteins
     and cells
     and molecules
     all are alive.

To move, indeed, is to be alive.
     Uli, motion,
     the sacred principle of
     ancient Mexico
     Uli, motion,
     produced first by the
     powers of the four directions
     who, being in disequilibrium,
     produced tension
     and the first movement
     the beginning of the physical universe
     as it would appear.

And indeed the astronomers know
     that there could be no
     first explosion
     no "big bang"

without movement
without motion
and only life moves
it is seen
the dead do not move.

Energy,
yes energy
we all have energy
and in our molecular cores
atomic centers
those ever-moving
electrons
particles
quarks
moving, moving, moving
alive, alive, alive!

Do you doubt still?
a rock alive? You say
it is hard!
it doesn't move of its own accord!
it has no eyes!
it doesn't think!
but rocks do move
put one in a fire
it will get hot won't it?
That means
won't you agree?
that its insides are moving
ever more rapidly?

Rocks are all different!
That one's not good for a sweat
because when it gets too
hot it will shatter!
It will fly all over the place
and burn you good!

And what about lava?
   Rocks flowing like water?
   And what about sand
   becoming rocks
   and what about sea shells
   and bones becoming rocks?

So don't kid me my friend,
   rocks change
   rocks move
   rocks flow
   rocks combine
   rocks are powerful friends
   I have many
   big and small
   their processes, at our temperatures,
   are very slow
   but very deep!

I understand because, you see,
   I am part rock!
   I eat rocks
   rocks are part of me
   I couldn't exist without
   the rock in me
   We are all related!

The mad materialists, of course,
   believe in blind faith
   that the elements are like machines
   that we have a mechanistic world
   where dead things combine
   magically
   as if on command
   as if commanded by a machine-maker
   as if programmed by a
   master programmer
   now assassinated of course!

But "mechanistic" can only be a metaphor
    a metaphor only possible
    during the past two centuries
    only possible in a factory
    where machines are made
    and placed and programmed.

Do we live in an auto-matic world
    where elements automatically combine
    where processes automatically occur?
    Well, auto-matic
    means self-acting
    and nothing self-acts if it is dead
    and we are all actors subject
    to heat
    to cold
    to pressure
    to attractions
    to rejections
    to instructions, and perhaps, at our electrical core,
    to chance.

And really, a world of machines,
    of dead, invariable combinings
    is a world which could never by itself change
    a static,
    frozen,
    dead world!

No, it's alive I tell you,
    just like the old ones say
    they've been there
    you know
    they've crossed the boundaries
    not with computers
    but with their
    very own beings!

Don't Ask Me To Believe It
(for Lorne Simon)

Don't ask me to believe it's true
don't ask me to believe
things like that can happen
to people
like me
and you

We shout words at one another
we place words into the air
trying to make them fit
somewhere
in the universe

We shoot words upward
into the endless black of space
wish that they find
particles of sparkling fire
and become stars
to guide the faded path
of one of our own

Searching for meaning
in this crazy place
of industry and spirit
we publish prophesy
rebirthing our nations
while it is those who surround us
who move toward their own end
by ignoring our words

So don't ask me to believe it's true

I picture you the dreaming moon
in a darkened Micmac sky
reflecting red off the northern lights
on the eastern seaboard
of this massive island

I picture you locking yourself up
with your computer
in a tiny room
that became a palace of words
a kingdom of pages
a universe of creation

You made yourself a jail
that became a prism of light
emanating every colour in the spectrum
through white and black

11 suicides in Big Cove
in the past two years
those young Micmac relatives
who were too battered
to find fulfilment in the fight
and you who lived to write

So don't ask me to believe it's true

You can not just go like that
without even asking me
to say good-bye
or tell of my respect
your talent
your dedication
your unbelievable stature
or your amazing words
the ones that make my own
seem like dribble
in TV commercials

Now we hold your book
open to the sky
calling you
to come back down
and read

We picture you locked up
in another room
writing new words into song
listening to new music
by Marley and Hendrix

And they are alive
I heard them just the other day
on the radio
and we have your book
and Heidi has your computer
and your computer has more books
waiting to be published

So don't ask me to believe it's true
don't ask me to believe
things like that can happen
to people
like me
and you

Children

AGE OF RAP

Those who once listened to
flutes and drums
Now listen to
rap
Driving in their
low-riding rez cars
That replaced
the proud ponies
They once rode
down to their tipi or
Their adobe
both brick and
Deer leather
give way to
Metal
mobile home
In the age of
rap

CLOUDS UNNOTICED

Light shades of grays mix, into the whites
The faintest hint of existing shadow.
Delicate, yet so bold.
It hovers, silently.
Constant action, yet still.
It lingers like the last words, of a love song.
Through the mind's eye it takes many forms.
Detached from all, apart.
Seen within, seen without
Parallel, with a sense of symmetry.
To all else, distant.
Distant, and yet so close.
To, and away.
A wanderer, a shadow thief.
Cascades of light it seals,
Radiant sunlight,
fiery reds and yellows and docile purples.
All fall about it,
As if it's calling them
Soft and sunken, mellow and light.
Gathered patches, weaving throughout
The clouds, glowing, and yet not.
A ferrying ark of the soul,
Whose picture perhaps tells a dream,
A tale,
A story of bright and dull wonder,
Sleepy, yet full awake
it's sitting, resting, there.
Against the blues,
Mellow and excited, It tugs at curiosity,
Pulls at imagination.
So different.
So similar.
In some strange sense,
A panorama of ones's self.
What one does, or does not see,
Perhaps it's a mirror to show,
All none,
None all.
It invokes thoughts of wonder.

Bluejay's Free Lunch

There once lived a young sneaky bluejay; he was the smartest bluejay of all the bluejays. All of the other bluejays didn't like lying around him because he was not only smart, but he was dishonest. So he usually travelled solo. But, he did not mind because he did not have to worry about others telling on him so it was easier to fool many.

One day when he flew off to find his lunch he saw a flock of robins below picking strawberries. As he soared towards the robins he thought of a way to trick his way into a free lunch. As he landed he pretended that he hurt his foot. He talked the robins into letting him watch their full baskets of berries. They weren't very sure at first, but he convinced them by saying that he had to rest his sore foot.

As soon as the robins were out of sight he immediately started devouring the berries. In no time he had eaten all of the berries, and realized that he had better come up with a plan quick because he could see the robins returning for their berries.

He quickly went over to a nearby strawberry plant and picked a few strawberries and smeared them all over his face to make it look like he was bleeding. So when the robins saw the empty basket and the blood (berry juice) on bluejay's face they felt sorry for him. They started asking him a bunch of questions like "What happened to your face? " and "Where did all of the berries go?" Bluejay replied saying "A seagull came and attacked me and took all of your berries. When the seagull attacked me it made my mouth bleed". Then bluejay said, "Here look my mouth is bleeding". As he showed them the red marks on his face.

The robins believed his story and felt sorry for him and offered him some of the strawberries that they had just picked. As he greedily ate these berries he soon started to get a stomach ache from eating too much.

The robins said, "We thought that you only hurt your foot and your mouth". "Yes" said bluejay. "I did hurt my foot and my mouth, but also I hurt my stomach when the crow took the berries". But, then the robins said, "You told us that it was a seagull". "Oh! Yes didn't I tell you that there was two birds" said bluejay.

That is when snail came creeping out of some bushes and said, "That's not true!" Snail told them the truth and, bluejay sadly flew home and went to bed with a stomach ache.

The moral of the story is ONE LIE LEADS TO ANOTHER AND IT IS ALWAYS BETTER TO TELL THE TRUTH

Nattie Parson's Good Luck Lamb

Once there was a little girl named Nattie. She lived with her grandma, and they had a small flock of sheep. One day Nattie found a small little lamb in the bushes. It had wirey and scragily wool. Nattie asked her grandma and she shook her head no. Nattie said she could be a good luck lamb. The grandma said all right we will call her Clover like a four leaf, said Nattie.

Then she fixed the lamb up in the barn and made her look clean and pretty. Whenever Clover wandered around she would get hungry, and she would go to the field and eat green leaves and grass.

Over the winter Nattie and Clover were so happy. They didn't see her grandma for a long time. But, then she came to Nattie and told Nattie that they don't have food for the winter. She said to last the winter we can only keep the sheep with the best wool. But, you won't sell Clover will you? asked Nattie. She can eat my food.

When it was bed time Nattie and Clover couldn't sleep. When Nattie went to pet Clover she was starving. So she went outside to get some raspberries. But, when Clover was going to stop eating the raspberries she saw one raspberry that she just couldn't pass by. So Clover ate all of the raspberries.

Nattie was calling Clover. Clover was looking for a smile on Nattie's face, but Nattie was upset because some of Clover's wool was stained from the raspberries that she had eaten. Then Nattie said, "Oh well I will just have to wash the wool until it comes out". Oh well thought Nattie that is the best I can do and it will just have to do the way it is.

Nattie was ready to use the sheep's wool for her weaving, and she started to work on her weaving right away.

Grandma went to the shop to sell the sheep that they had ready for the market, and Nattie had her weaving in a bag ready to sell as well. When they got to the store Nattie told the store owner that she had woven a shawl to sell. The store owner said that the shawl might not be suitable to sell in this store.

Then Nattie pulled the shawl from her bag just as two rich people came through the door. One of them said that Nattie had a fine weaving. The other person took the weaving from Nattie and said that they would buy the weaving for what ever amount it is worth. So Nattie sold the weaving and the money lasted them for the rest of the winter. Nattie said that maybe next time Clover could eat the blueberries and the wool for the shawl could be blue instead of pink like it was this time from the raspberries that Clover had eaten that stained the wool.

How The Halibut Got It's Shape

It was many years ago in a small bay called Kitgoro. There was a young halibut. He was very heavy and very strong. He had a lot of confidence.. a bit too much. He always teased all the other creatures in the bay. He was told not to go near the surface. He was wondering why he should not go to the surface. He was told if he went to the surface that he would be attacked by many dangerous creatures like hawks, eagles and otters. Seals were the most dangerous of all.

Kitgoro is a very plentiful place and there were lots of eagles, seals and otters. It is a very dangerous place in Kitgoro. The halibut was very daring and fast. He thought that he could outrun anything that would try to attack him but what he did not know was how fast and strong the eagles were.

The halibut was very bored one day. He decided to go to the surface. He went up for about 5 minutes and finally got to the surface. When he got there he poked his head out of the water but just as fast as he had poked his head out of the water he went back in. Then he poked his head out of the water but this time he did not go back down. He was looking at the amazing scenery. He was amazed by the bright light. Where he had come from it was always very dark. After awhile he was getting tired. He decided to find some herring to eat and then go home. He wanted to tell his friends but he knew if someone found out that he had gone to the surface, he would have gotten into a lot of trouble.

He made many trips to the surface. He found lots of different things on the surface. When spring came to Kitgoro he was going to the surface more frequently.

The one trip that he made to the surface that he would never forget was about halfway through the summer: He was swimming on the surface when all of a sudden an eagle came swooping out of the sky and grabbed him and flew away. The eagle was very big and strong...very strong! At first the eagle wasn't very tired and he was heading to shore very quickly. After awhile he was getting tired. He had grabbed the halibut in his left eye. The halibut was in a lot pain and he did not have a lot of time to get out of the eagle's grasp. The halibut was very frantic. The eagle was slowing down a bit but not very much. The eagle wasn't loosening his grip at all. The halibut was getting to the point that he was hardly able to think straight. The halibut was getting very tired but he was keeping himself from falling unconscious. He was trying to find a way to get out of the eagles's grasp. He had been in a lot of pain but he held on to the one hope that the eagle would get tired and drop him into the ocean. Then he would have to get passed the seals and otters.

It had been a long time and the eagle was getting very close to shore. The rocks were very jagged but there was a flat spot. It was too far from the water. There was a small stream. He didn't have much time. He had to get out of the eagle's grasp very soon! The eagle was getting so tired that he could hardly hold on to the halibut. He was right over the creek bed. All of a sudden the eagle could not hold on any longer. The halibut started to go unconscious and the last thing that he could remember was hitting the creek bed and feeling his ribs smash to the sides of his body. Then he went unconscious. The halibut was washed out to sea so fast that the seals did not have time to notice him. He revived about an hour later with an unbearable pain in his ribs. He could not swim. Then he noticed what had happened to him. He was as flat as the ocean floor and he had only one eye. He tried to move but he could not. His ribs had pierced his sides. They stuck out about an inch and a half.

In about a year these ribs grew fins on the tips of them . It took him about 2 weeks before he could swim again. He did not live very happily. He was never able to get into any of the good feeding spots because he was always chased away.

From that day forth the halibut lays flat on the bottom of the ocean and never comes to the surface.

Biographies

Nelson J. Augustine is a member of the MicMac First Nation at Big Cove, New Brunswick. He was a student and the En'owkin Centre in 1991-92. He is currently employed by the Big Cove Band Council as a technical writer and program coordinator. Nelson is planning to write several full-length novels, one of which will include the passage, Joshua and the Troop Leader, and the other he will co-author with another MicMac individual.

Melissa Austin is 13 years old and she is from the Tsarlip Band on Vancouver Island just north of Victoria. Melissa lives with her sister, Alison who is 10 years old, and with her mother, Sheilia. Melissa attends Bayside Middle School in Brentwood Bay. She enjoys school a lot.

Rodney Bobiwash is an Anishinabe (Ojibway) from the Thessaon Reserve on the north shore of Lake Huron, in Northern Ontario. Rodney attended high school north of Sudbury and studied Native Studies at Trent University in Peterborough and Commonwealth and Imperial History at Oxford University in England. Rodney has been a lecturer in the Native Studies Department at the University of Manitoba and Trent University, worked at the Indian Commission of Ontario, the Native Canadian Centre of Toronto, and the Congress of Aboriginal People in Ottawa. He is a community activist and organizer who has worked, written and spoken extensively in the areas of self-government, anti racist strategies and hate groups, employment equity and Native rights. He is currently the Director of First Nations House at the University of Toronto.

Bill Cohen is a member of the Okanagan Nation. He attended the University of Lethbridge. He was published in Volume II of Gatherings. He is also the illustrator for Jordan Wheeler's book *Just A Walk*, published by Theytus Books. Bill is currently teaching En'owkin Centre's Adult Basic Education program at Westbank, B.C.

Frank Conibear is from the Lyackson Band (Coast Salish) on Valdez Island. He grew up and lives in Victoria, B.C. He is a teacher/counselor at Esquimalt Secondary, working primarily with First Nation students. Frank has been published in *Volume IV of Gatherings*.

Kateri Damm is a member of the Chippewas of Nawash, Cape Croker Band on Georgian Bay, Ontario and is of mixed Ojibway/Polish Canadian/Pottawotami/English descent. She was born in Toronto. *My Heart Is A Stray Bullet* was her first collection of poetry. Kateri was published in *Volume V of Gatherings*.

Jack Forbes is the Director of Native Studies at the University of California, his tribal affiliations are Delware-Lenpa and Powhantan-Renape. He is the author of many books including, *Columbus and Cannibals*. Jack is published in *Volume V of Gatherings*.

Raven Hail is an active member of the Cherokee Nation. Her poetry and essays on Cherokee culture have appeared in various publications. She has also written three novels and a cook book. Raven has been published in Volume V of Gatherings.

A.A. Hedge Coke: is of mixed-blood (Huron; Tsalagi; French Canadian;Portuguese) She is currently a corresponding student in the MFA in Writing program at Vermont College. Her full-length poetry manuscript is being retained by a leading press, her full-length play is a finalist in a major competition, and her novel in progress is a semi-finalist in line for a workshop fellowship,

Travis Hedge Coke is fourteen years old and is the son of A.A. Hedge Coke.

Jose Garza (Blue Heron) is of Coahuilteca/Mexican and Lipan Apache heritage. He lives in western Pennsylvania. Jose has been published in *Volume V of Gatherings*.

Barbara-Helen Hill is from Six Nations Grand River Territory, located in southern Ontario. She is presently a student at the En'owkin Centre. Barbara-Helen has completed a manuscript entitled: *Shaking the Rattle*, which will be published by Theytus Books.

Debby Keeper is a Cree from the Fisher River First Nation in the Interlake area of Manitoba. Debby is a visual artist and has been published in *Volume V of Gatherings*.

Randy Lundy is of of Cree, Irish, Norwegian and Scottish descent. His maternal roots lie in Northern Manitoba, along the eastern shores of Reindeer Lake. He grew up in Hudson Bay, Saskatchewan and has been living in Saskatoon since the fall of 1987. Randy is currently enrolled in a Master of Arts program in English and plan to complete a thesis on Native Literature.

Melvina B. Mack aka Nuxilhtimut is from the Nuxalkmc Nation on the north coast of B.C. She has very recently completed the two year term of Creative Writing at En'owkin International School of Writing at Penticton, B.C. Her future endeavors are to return home for a spell before continuing on to the University of Victoria.

Victoria Lena Manyarrows is Tsalagi/Eastern Cherokee and 39 years old. She was raised alongside reservations and within communities in North Dakota and Nebraska. As a writer, activist and artist, her goal is to use written and visual images to convey and promote a positive Native-based world view. Victoria's essays and poetry have been published in various Native and multicultural publications in the United States and Canada.

Henry Michel is Secwepemc from the Sugar Cane Reserve in central B.C. Henry has three poems published in *Seventh Generation*, Theytus Books Ltd. and one poem in *Voices Under One Sky*, Nelson Canada Ltd. Henry is also published in *Volume V of Gatherings.*

Tiffany Midge is a member of the Standing Rock Sioux Reservation and has lived for the majority of her 29 years in the Seattle area. Some of her previous publication credits include, *Cutbank, The Ark, Blue Mesa Review* and *The Raven Chronicles*. Her first collection of poetry, *Outlaws, Renegades & Saints: Diary of a Mixed-Up Halfbreed* was the recipient of the 1994 Diane Decorah Memorial Poetry Award from the Native Writer's Circle of the Americas, and will be published in late '95 by Greenfield Review Press.

Daniel David Moses is a Delaware poet and playwright from the Six Nations lands on the Grand River in Southern Ontario. His publications include the play *Coyote City* (Williams & Wallace 1990), and the book of poems *The White Line* (Fifth House 1990) and was the co-editor of *An Anthology of Canadian Native Literature in English* (Oxford 1992). Daniel has also been published in Gatherings Vol. 3 (Theytus Books 1992).

Jacqueline Oker is a Beaver Indian from the Doig River Reserve near Fort St. John, B.C. Jackie has been published in *Volume V of Gatherings*.

Brenda Prince is Anishinabe from Winnipeg, Manitoba. She is mother of Raven, Robin and Dakota. She is a second year student at the En'owkin International School of Writing.

Sharron Proulx is a member of the Metis Nation of Alberta (Mohawk, Huron, Algonquin, French and Irish ancestors). Sharron's working on a book of stories and poems called *she is reading her blanket with her hands*.

Armand Garnet Ruffo is Ojibway from Chapleau, Northern Ontario. He currently divides his time between Northern Ontario, Ottawa, where he is the Associate Director of the Centre of Aboriginal Education Research and Culture, and Penticton, B.C. where he is an instructor at the En'owkin International School of writing. Armand's first book of poetry *Opening In The Sky,* has been published by Theytus Books Ltd.

Strong Morning Sky is from the Ojibway and Mic Mac Nation and is currently attending the University of Winnipeg. Her poem was written in memory of Anna Mae Aquash and Helen Betty Osborne.

Russell Teed is a Metis from Yellowknife, NWT. He has graduated from the En'owkin International School of Writing in Penticton where he founded and co-edited the Newsletter *Tee-Pee Talk.* He also co-edited the Theytus anthology *Webs of Wisdom*. In 1993/94 he won the Simon Lucas Jr. scholarship, and in 1994/95 he won the William Armstrong scholarship for fiction. Russell is currently editing his first manuscript of short stories.

Judith Mtn. Leaf Volborth: is of Blackfeet/Comanche descent. She has been published in numerous periodicals, anthologies and magazines. Judith has also been featured in *Volume II of Gatherings*.

Other Contributors:
Annie Bosum
Isabelle Louise Hill
Dona F. Lewis
Josh Nelson
Dawne Starfire
Laurie Weahkee
Greg Young-Ing